WABASH CARNEGIE P LIB

W9-BLT-643

POINTS

9.0

YA Fic Hrd
Hrdlitschka, Shelley
Dancing naked

sys00041936

DISCARD

WABASH CARNEGIE PUBLIC LIBRARY

WABASH CARNEGIE PUBLIC LIBRARY

Dancing naked

A NOVEL

SHELLEY HRDLITSCHKA

ORCA BOOK PUBLISHERS

Copyright © 2001 Shelley Hrdlitschka

All rights reserved. No part of this publication may be
reproduced or transmitted in any form or by any
means, electronic or mechanical, including
photocopying, recording or by any information storage
and retrieval system now known or to be invented,
without permission in writing from the publisher.

National Library of Canada Cataloguing in Publication Data
Hrdlitschka, Shelley, 1956-

Dancing naked

ISBN 1-55143-210-2

1. Teenage pregnancy–Fiction. 2. Adoption–Fiction. I. Title.

PS8565.R44D35 2001   jC813'.54   C2001-910946-6

PZ7.H854Da 2001

First published in the United States, 2002

Library of Congress Catalog Card Number: 2001092678

Orca Book Publishers gratefully acknowledges the support for
its publishing programs provided by the following agencies:
the Government of Canada through the Book Publishing Industry
Development Program (BPIDP), the Canada Council
for the Arts, and the British Columbia Arts Council.

Cover design: Christine Toller
Cover photograph: Image Copyright © Digital Vision

Printed and bound in Canada

IN CANADA:
Orca Book Publishers
PO Box 5626, Station B
Victoria, BC Canada
V8R 6S4

IN THE UNITED STATES:
Orca Book Publishers
PO Box 468
Custer, WA USA
98240-0468

03 02 01 • 5 4 3 2

To Heather Verrier, sister and dear friend.

Acknowledgements

A huge thank you to: Reverend Brian Kiely for so graciously creating an adoption ceremony and then allowing me to tamper with it at will; Diane Tullson, who inspired the title and prodded me into writing the book; and the members of my Tuesday and Thursday morning writing groups for their enthusiasm and ongoing support, despite my lousy attendance record.

I'm particularly indebted to Beryl Young, Kim Denman, Alice Frampton, Sandra Diersch, Alison Harvey, Amanda Harvey, Vivienne Frampton and Kate Blake, who read early drafts of the manuscript and whose comments and suggestions were invaluable. The lyrics to the song on page 227 were written by Alice Frampton and are used with permission.

I'm blessed by my association with the Unitarian church, and the creators of the O.W.L. (Our Whole Lives) program, for the inspiration that flavors this story.

Finally, I'd like to thank Andrew Wooldridge of Orca Book Publishers, for understanding—from the start—what it is to dance naked, and for the wise guidance, humor and insight that he brings to the editing process.

prologue

The spirit of life dances lightly among the people gathered in the birthing room, teasing goosebumps to the surface of their skin, forcing fine hairs to stand at attention. It is elusive, silent and indefinable, yet they all feel its mysterious presence, its promise, as it swirls about, waiting to breathe the silent respiration of the universe into the newest member of the human family.

The birth begins as small, regular and almost painless contractions that remind the girl of soft ocean waves gently lapping the shore. She is able to relax and accept them, knowing, just as with ocean waves, there is nothing she can do to stop the continuous ebb and flow. But they gradually increase in intensity, just as waves increase in strength with an oncoming storm. They begin to peak, and in the girl's mind they've become whitecaps, slapping the shore, boasting of their power and volume and hinting that the worst is yet to come. *Just try to make us go away,* they seem to say when she longs to stop and turn the calendar back nine months to a time when she can make different choices, when she still has options. But the contractions continue to rip through her and she feels like she is being battered by the storm—the waves are smashing against the shore and she is no longer able to focus or see the reason for being there. She is losing her breath, drowning in pain.

Suddenly she's shaking all over. A low moaning comes from deep within her. Someone says it is time, time to push. *You're ready*, the voice says. But she already knows that. With a desire and strength that surprises her, she leans forward and bears down, joining with—instead of fighting against—the unrelenting forces of nature. She is vaguely aware of chanting voices. *Push, push, push*, the voices say. The moaning becomes a cat-like howl and then fevered panting. She is totally focused on the task at hand. The other people in the room no longer exist for her. There is only the overwhelming need to push, the excruciating pain and the throbbing new life inside her that wants to be born.

The room spins and sweat drips into her eyes. She feels an unearthly power assisting her and she continues to bear down with each crashing wave. The storm crests and she feels an explosion, like a volcanic eruption. *The head is born!* someone declares. A few more pushes and then the baby slides out with a gush of blood and fluid that pools around her. The tiny baby is placed on her bare belly, its airways are suctioned, and the umbilical cord is severed. For a moment she feels a pang of grief, for now she is only one again; there are no longer two hearts beating inside her. But she pushes the grief aside and watches as the baby inhales deeply, drawing in air, that final yet vital life force. Then it begins to wail, a raw and insistent cry, and the sound fills the girl with awe.

The crashing waves subside quickly. The storm has passed, but in its passing it has blessed the earth with a new life whose spirit is now a tangible and very noisy presence.

the first trimester

Kia stepped into her flannel, teddy bear-speckled boxer shorts and tugged one of her dad's old T-shirts over her head. Crossing the room to turn off the overhead light, she caught a glimpse of herself in the full-length mirror. She paused and stared at her reflection, her dark eyes resting on her waist and stomach. She pulled the T-shirt up and the waistband of the shorts down for a closer inspection. Turning sideways but still looking in the mirror, she let go of the waistband and ran her hand over her stomach. It was flat and firm, same as always. Using both hands she slowly pulled the T-shirt up higher, exposing her chest. A loose strand of long hair tickled the soft, sensitive skin. Her breasts looked the same, but she knew that something was different. She let go of her T-shirt with one hand and gently pressed the soft flesh. Her breast felt bruised and sore, even though there was no outward sign of injury.

Hearing a movement in the hall, she dropped her shirt, blushing at the thought of being caught studying her own body. She flicked the light switch and climbed into bed. The reading lamp cast a pool of light onto her night table. Pulling open a drawer, she reached for the tattered notebook she used as a journal, but hesitated before taking it out. Instead, she picked up the beautiful spiral-bound book that lay on top of the table and ran her hand across its cover. It was made from recycled paper, and seeds and delicate flower petals were pressed into it. She leafed through the pages; each one was unique, flecked with bits of pastel-colored tissue that had bled, creating a mottled effect. Though they felt slightly grainy to the touch, the pages seemed as delicate as butterfly wings as she turned them.

Shawna had given her the journal for Christmas because she knew about Kia's compulsive journal-writing habit; she was the only person allowed to read what Kia wrote. Shawna was also the only person who knew what she'd done with Derek. Once. But, of course, once is all it takes.

Kia hadn't written in the journal yet, not wanting to mar its unspoiled beauty. She opened the cover and re-read the inscription.

> To my wise friend Kia. Your words deserve special paper.
> Keep on writing girl!
> Luv ya,
> Shawna

She continued to turn the pages, undecided, then saw a connection between what was on her mind and the new journal. Picking up her pen, she turned to the first page and began to write.

> Jan. 1
> Virgin paper, fresh, crisp, clean
> Is only an illusion.
> It's recycled, not pure at all.

Illusion ... do I look different?
Can anyone see what is happening to me?

Kia skimmed over what she'd written. She shook her head, surprised, as usual, at what had appeared on the page. She put the journal in her night table, turned off the light and snuggled down under her comforter, but she knew sleep would elude her again tonight. She curled herself into a fetal position and allowed her thoughts to return to that night, just five weeks ago. The night that had changed her life, possibly forever.

From: Justin <justintime@yahoo.com>
To: Kia <hazelnut@hotmail.com>
Date: Jan. 3
Subject: r u ok?

hey kia, there was someone who looked just like u at youth group last night but i guess it wasn't u. she wouldn't look at me, she said "pass" at her turn in check-in and she looked majorly out-of-sorts.

what's up?
justin

From: Kia <hazelnut@hotmail.com>
To: Justin <justintime@yahoo.com>
Date: Jan. 3
Subject: Re: r u ok?

justin, i'm sorry about my lousy mood @ youth group. it's not u and it's not the group. i can't share it yet, but it's ... i don't know. maybe i'll be able 2 talk about it later, maybe not.

kia

From: Justin <justintime@yahoo.com>
To: Kia <hazelnut@hotmail.com>
Date: Jan. 3
Subject: all ears

kia,

i'm here 2 listen when you're ready to talk about it. u'll feel better, guaranteed. (that's why they pay us youth group advisors the big bucks!)

T.O.Y.
justin

Kia watched as Derek leaned over the pool table, lining up a shot. "Are you about done playing with yourself?"

Derek glanced up from the billiard balls, his pale blue eyes meandering up the length of her body before reaching her eyes. Her black hair was caught up in a butterfly clip, and it fanned out over her shoulders as she lay sprawled on the couch. "Very funny, Kia," he said. "And as you know, I'd rather play with you any day." He took the shot, then turned back to her, his seductive smile spreading slowly across his face. That smile alone usually created a stir throughout her entire being, but not tonight. Her stomach was stirring, but for other reasons.

"You're looking a little pale," he said, hanging his pool cue on the wall. "Are you sure you're over that flu thing?"

"I didn't have the flu."

"No?" He settled himself down on the couch beside her. "Just skipping school? That's not like you." He leaned over, his lips lightly brushing hers while his hand ran down her arm, over her hip and began its way up her back, under her sweater. She was tempted to give in to the flood of wonderful sensations, that full-body rush. There was none of that clumsy, pawing stuff with Derek. He knew what he was doing. But that's how she'd gotten into this mess in the first place.

"Derek." Kia pulled away before he could unhook her bra. She reached for his hand—to keep it off her—and began massaging his palm. Her thumbs dug deep into his flesh. She waited until he made eye contact with her. "We have a problem."

"Really."

Kia could see he didn't care.

"It can wait. It's been way too long." His eyes looked like hazy blue pools as he leaned forward to kiss her again.

She had more willpower this time. "No, Derek."

He sat back with a sigh. "It's *that* time of the month, right?"

Kia almost laughed at the irony. "No, that's not it."

"Oh, good." The smile was back, but now it was looking more mischievous than sexy. "Everyone's out," he said. "Why don't we help ourselves to a couple bottles of beer and find somewhere more comfortable to hang out? Then, when we get back to this," he ran his finger lightly along her bottom lip, "it will be even better." He leaned forward to kiss her again, but she pushed him away. She hated that he could still make her want more, even now.

She stood up and walked toward the pool table. "*This* is the problem, Derek."

"This? What are you talking about?" He looked confused. Or was it angry?

She took a deep breath and let it spill out. "You knew

I didn't want to … to go all the way. But you said it was safe, you had a condom, but …"

"But what?" He actually looked puzzled, as if he couldn't see where she was going with this.

"I think I'm pregnant."

Derek stared at her, stunned. She stared back. The desire that she'd just seen in his eyes had vanished, and they looked hard and flat. She noticed his jaw clenching. He finally found his voice. "You say you think. You don't know for sure?"

"Right. But I'm almost three weeks late."

"That's it?" Derek brushed by her. He grabbed the pool cue from the hook on the wall. "I hear my sisters talking all the time. That's no big deal."

"It's a big deal for me. I'm never late. Haven't been since I started in grade seven. That's five years without changing."

Derek lined up his shot. "You haven't taken a test or something?"

"No."

The cue ball slammed into the colored balls. They spun away in every direction, but it didn't look like any of them were going to sink into the pockets. Kia watched the cue ball. It rolled slowly toward a corner pocket and dropped in.

"Shit!" Derek flung the pool cue onto the table and turned to her. "Then take one. You can get them at the drugstore, cheap. And don't bother me again until you know for sure." He stormed out of the room and Kia heard him stomp down the hall. Then she heard the footsteps returning. She felt a rush of relief. He was going to apologize. He was just upset.

He stood in the doorway, glaring at her. "And don't give me any of that crap about it being all my fault." He spat the words out. "You wanted to do it as much as I did." He spun around and thumped back down the hallway, his bedroom door slamming behind him.

Kia stared at the empty doorway, shocked. Don't bother him? That was it? "Fuck you, Derek Klassen!" she yelled, hurling a cushion through the doorway. But he was right, she realized as she slipped into her shoes and left though the front door. She had wanted to do it. That was the part she hated most.

Jan. 5
Blue.
The blue of tropical water, the surf pounding the shore.
The blue of the sky on a brilliant spring day.
The blue of a speckled robin's egg.
The ice-blue of Derek's eyes.
The blue ring in the water.
It's confirmed.
I am.
Blue.

The phone rang four times before he picked it up.

"Derek. It's me, Kia."

"Uh-huh." There was not even a trace of warmth in his voice.

"I took the test."

"And?"

"It's positive. I am."

For a second Kia thought the phone had gone dead. Then she heard him whisper, "Shit."

"Exactly."

"Okay." Derek cleared his throat. "Here's what we have to do. I'll take you to a clinic tomorrow after school. We'll get it confirmed at a lab. Those home jobs aren't always accurate. It could be wrong."

Kia knew it wasn't wrong, but she didn't argue. She was relieved that he was taking charge, and he was right, they did have to rule out any doubt.

"Make sure you have your health insurance number with you," he added.

"Okay. And then?"

"Then, if we have to, we go to a different kind of clinic."

"You sound like you've got experience with this stuff." Kia rolled her eyes. It figured.

"I wasn't born yesterday."

"Do you want to do something this afternoon?" Maybe he could redeem himself—a little—by showing even the teeniest streak of compassion. At least pretend that he cared about her and how she felt.

"Do something?"

"Yeah." Like get together and cry on each other's shoulder, she thought. "Hang out, go for a drive. You know, do something."

"Sorry, Kia. I've got too much homework."

Homework? It was a well-known fact that Derek Klassen never did homework.

"Fine." She hung up before he had a chance to say anything else, but there wasn't the usual satisfaction in getting in the last word. There was only a rush of anger—mostly at herself. How could she have been so stupid?

~

Kia logged onto the Internet. She tapped in the word *pregnancy*. A moment later a list with over 500,000 sites was displayed. Starting at the top, she read the headings until she came to one called *Week to Week Pregnancy Calendar*. She pointed the cursor to it and clicked.

The site came up. She scanned the information and then hit the print command. While she waited for the hard copy, she did some quick calculations. If a pregnancy lasts forty weeks from the first day of the last menstrual cycle, that made her seven weeks pregnant already!

Snatching the pages off the printer, Kia went down the hall to her room. After shutting the door, she glanced down the page until she came to the entry for seven weeks. She read:

The leg and arm buds have begun to appear. The brain is growing and developing. The heart has divided into right and left chambers. The eyes and nostrils are developing, as are the intestines, appendix and pancreas. All this, yet it is only the size of a green pea.

Hearing the front door bang open, Kia folded the pages and quickly tucked them into her journal.

~

"Which clinic are we going to?" Kia yelled over the din of the boom box.

"Over on the East Side," Derek yelled back. "Don't

want to run into anyone we know."

Kia nodded and sat back in the passenger seat of his '78 Chevy Impala. She watched the windshield wipers slap back and forth. The heater in his car didn't work, so she pulled her jacket together and began to fold her arms across her chest, but that made her wince, her breasts were so sore.

Glancing at Derek as he sang along with his favorite rapper, Kia saw him check his reflection in the rear-view mirror, lick his fingers and smooth his already perfectly groomed hair. Then he went back to tapping out rhythms on the steering wheel, except when he was honking or giving another driver the finger, which he seemed to do every few blocks, just as a matter of principle. Kia looked away. Why hadn't these things irritated her before?

They pulled into a Superstore parking lot. Kia saw the sign for the walk-in clinic to the right of the main entrance. She was beginning to think Derek had been here before; he knew exactly where to go.

The woman at the front desk told Kia to add her name to the long list on the clipboard and to have a seat. The waiting room was full; the only two vacant chairs were across the room from one another. Derek plunked himself in one, picked up a *Sports Illustrated* and began to flip through it. Kia sank into the remaining chair. On her right, an elderly man coughed hard, a phlegmy, rattling noise coming from his chest. She turned, putting her back to him just in time to see the small boy with a crusty nose on her left strike his baby sister in the face with a toy truck. The baby hollered, the mother smacked the little boy, and he gave a blood-curdling scream.

Kia stood up and went back to the desk. "How long do you think the wait will be?" she asked.

The woman smiled sympathetically, but shook her head. "It's hard to judge," she said. "Could be as long as forty-five minutes." She placed a clipboard in front of Kia. "You might as well fill this out while you're waiting."

Kia took her time filling in her medical history. When she got to the last question, she paused. *Reason for today's visit*, it asked. She looked over at Derek, who was still engrossed in the magazine. She considered putting *vasectomy for boyfriend* in the blank space, but didn't feel like using the word "boyfriend." She sighed and wrote in *pregnancy test*.

Each minute seemed an hour long. Kia paced across the front of the waiting room. The sneezing, sniffling and coughing were as incessant as the whining of the small children. She stepped outside and breathed in lungfuls of the damp air, hesitant to return to the stuffy, germ-filled room.

When her name was finally called, she glanced at Derek, expecting him to join her as she followed the nurse down the hall to the examining room. But he didn't move, just stared back at her. She went alone.

The person who burst into the tiny room after what seemed like another hour didn't look nearly old enough to be a doctor, but she shook Kia's hand and introduced herself as Dr. Aya Miyata. She glanced down at the form Kia had filled out.

"So you think you're pregnant."

"Yes. I know I am. I took a home test, it was positive, and I feel gross. My breasts hurt. I know that's how you feel when you get pregnant."

"And how do you know that?"

Kia studied the doctor's face, wondering if what she was really asking was whether she'd been pregnant before. "I took a human sexuality class at church," she answered defensively. "We discussed pregnancy."

"At church?"

"Uh-huh."

"I guess sex could be viewed as a religious experience," the doctor teased.

Kia shrugged. "My church is known for being kind of liberal."

"Liberal? What else did you discuss at this course?"

Kia narrowed her eyes. "No, teenagers are not encouraged to have sex, if that's what you're asking. But we are given all the facts so we can make informed choices."

"That's not what I was asking," the doctor responded gently. "But I am glad to hear someone is providing teens with all the facts."

Kia just nodded. She regretted snapping at the doctor.

"And you obviously chose to have sex."

"Obviously."

"You are ... how old?" Kia could see her trying to figure it out from the birth date written on the form.

"I'm almost seventeen."

The doctor smiled. "Almost seventeen. I like the way kids always tell you what age they almost are."

Kia didn't reply.

"But I guess you're not a kid if you're pregnant," the doctor said quietly, looking hard at Kia.

"Yeah, well, a lot of little grade seven kids are capable

of having babies, but they're not adults."

"Good point." She nodded, still studying Kia thoughtfully. "So where's the father?" she asked.

"In the waiting room."

"Really? What's he doing there?"

"I don't know. Sitting."

"What's his name?"

"Derek."

"Excuse me. I'll be right back." Kia could hear the doctor's heels click as she marched down the hall to the waiting room. Then she heard her say, "Derek? Could you please identify yourself?" A moment later Dr. Miyata re-appeared at the door, followed by a sullen-looking Derek.

"Have a seat," the doctor said.

Derek refused to look at Kia as he plunked himself in the other chair.

"So," the doctor said to Derek, "Kia's pregnant."

Suddenly Derek did look at Kia. Then he turned to the doctor. "Have you already given her the test?"

"No, but Kia's already one hundred percent certain that she is and I'm ninety percent sure that she's right. Have you considered what you're going to do when it's been confirmed by a lab test?"

"What are you talking about?" Derek sounded in-credulous. "I'm seventeen, she's sixteen, so there's nothing to consider. She has to get an abortion."

"Yes, abortion is one choice," the doctor said. "There's also adoption, or parenthood."

Derek scoffed. "Why would you try to talk a six-teen-year-old kid into having a baby? It can't be good for her."

"I'm not trying to talk her into anything. But you have to make an informed decision, and abortion is not necessarily good for her either," Dr. Miyata said. "It can leave emotional scars, and as with any medical procedure, there are risks."

Derek shook his head. "Just give her the test, and then we'll deal with it, okay?"

"Why weren't you using birth control?" the doctor asked.

"That's none of your business," Derek blurted out, glancing sharply at Kia. "But if you must know," he added, turning back to the doctor, "we were. I'm not stupid. We used a condom."

Dr. Miyata tilted her head. "So what happened?"

"I dunno. We must be that lucky one percent or whatever it is." He shrugged. "And we only did it once."

"I think that magic number is quite a bit higher than one percent," the doctor commented. "And it doesn't matter how many times you do it. Nothing is one hundred percent effective—nothing but abstinence." She scribbled something on her pad of paper, ripped the sheet off and handed it to Kia. "You need to go to a lab to get the test. Here's the address and requisition. Call me tomorrow to get the results."

Kia took the sheet and glanced at the scrawled handwriting.

"And don't forget, Kia," the doctor added as she stood up. "Your opinion in all this counts too."

Kia could see Derek's jaw clench again. She nodded, swallowing hard. "I know."

The lab was a few blocks away. Derek squealed

around the corners and blasted his horn at every car that dared drive in front of him.

"Why don't you just stick a picture of your middle finger in the window?" Kia asked. "It would save you a lot of trouble."

"Shut up," he snarled. "No one asked you."

⌒

Fifteen minutes later, Kia came out of the lab and climbed into the idling car where Derek sat waiting. He threw the car into gear and left a long slash of rubber on the pavement as he drove out of the parking lot. Kia pulled her seat belt more tightly over her shoulder.

Just before reaching her home, Derek pulled into the driveway of the elementary school they'd both attended. He'd been a year ahead of her, but Kia had known who he was. He'd had a reputation, even back then. He brought the car to a screeching stop in the empty staff parking lot.

"Who else knows you're late?" he asked.

"No one."

"Good. Keep it that way."

"Don't worry." Kia glared at him. "You're not something I'm real proud of." She shook her head. "One minute you're kissing me, getting all psyched up to do it again, and the next you're treating me like I have some kind of STD. Oh, yeah, like I chose a real winner to do it with. Can't wait to tell everyone I know."

"You were hot for me."

"Yeah, well, my brain and my body weren't connecting."

He studied her, his eyes narrowed. "You know," he said finally, "you and I could have been good together.

You're freaking gorgeous and for a first-timer you showed potential. Too bad."

Kia stared at him, speechless. Then, still without a word, she climbed out of the car, slammed the door and stormed away in the drizzling rain.

When she got home she went straight to her room and pulled her new journal out of the drawer. She stared at a blank page. The perfect words eluded her, but she was determined to express her feelings somehow. She remembered a silly curse she'd once heard. She wrote it down, read it over, then revised it.

Jan. 10
May the fleas of a thousand camels infest his Tommy Hilfiger jockey shorts.
No, a swarm of bees—same place.

She put the journal away, feeling only slightly better but knowing Shawna, at least, would enjoy that entry.

~

"Kia?"

Kia shook her head slightly. "Huh?" They were walking along the sidewalk on their way home from school.

Shawna stared at her, puzzled. "Are you okay? You didn't answer my question."

"Sorry. What did you ask?"

"What's the matter?"

"What's the matter? That's what you asked me?"

"No," Shawna said. "That's not what I asked you before, but that's what I'm asking you now. You haven't heard a word I've said all the way home. So now I want to know, what's the matter?"

Kia stared at her feet as they walked. She could usually tell Shawna anything, but not this. Not yet. Not until after she made the phone call and it was confirmed. But she could give her part of the story. "It's Derek. He's being a jerk."

Shawna glanced at her. "So, what else is new?"

"Thanks, Shawn. You're a big help."

"Sorry, Kia." Shawna turned and walked backwards, so she could face Kia. The wind blew strands of her long, light brown hair into her face. "But all along I've been worried he'd hurt you. You knew that."

Kia didn't reply. She didn't want to hear this again. She began to walk a little faster.

Shawna turned and picked up her pace too. "C'mon, Kia. I said I was sorry. Tell me what happened."

Kia shook her head. "Nothing. Except that I think he's dumping me."

"Did he *say* he wanted to break up?"

"No. Not in those words." Kia thought back to what he had said. *You and I could have been good together.* "But he made it clear. And I guess he'd never made any commitment to me in the first place," she added quietly.

"Kia, I'm sorry. I know you really liked him. Liked him enough to …" She left the sentence unfinished.

That reminded Kia of the phone call she had to make.

They had reached her driveway, and Kia stopped, crossed her arms and faced Shawna. "You're not sorry at all. You never even liked him."

Shawna flushed and narrowed her eyes. "You're right. I think he's an arrogant prick. And he never sticks with one girlfriend very long. *You* know that." Her voice softened.

"But what I think doesn't matter. You like him and I hate seeing you hurt. I know how it feels to get dumped."

"I thought Derek and I had something different going on." Kia couldn't meet Shawna's eyes. "Something special."

"Did you really believe that?" Shawna asked quietly. "Given his track record?"

"Yeah, I did. But I wouldn't expect you to understand, Shawna." Kia abruptly turned away and started up her driveway, blinking back tears. "I gotta go," she called over her shoulder. "See ya."

She quickly let herself into the house, trying to push away the meanness that was gnawing at her like a flesh-eating disease. All she could think about was how she wanted to hurt Shawna, for being right. But she had a phone call she had to make, and she had to make it now, before anyone else got home. She'd deal with Shawna later.

Pulling the doctor's phone number out of her pocket, Kia picked up the phone and, her hand shaking, began to punch in the numbers. She stopped before hitting the last one. She put the phone back in its cradle. Her pounding heart felt like it was wedged in her throat, threatening to choke her. There was no way she'd be able to speak. She wiped her hands on her jeans and sat down, breathing deeply. Then, when she felt her heart had settled enough for her to talk, she tried again. The phone rang once, twice, three times.

"Hello. Fairview Medical Clinic. How may I help you?"

Kia cleared her throat. "Hi. Yeah. This is Kia Hazelwood. I was in …".

The receptionist cut her off. "Yes, Kia. The results from your test came in this afternoon. Can I set up an appointment for you with the doctor?"

"No. Just give me the results."

"I'm sorry, Kia, I'm not at liberty to give that kind of information out over the phone. How about if I get the doctor to call you?"

Kia struggled to maintain her temper and to keep her voice steady. "But I need to know. Today."

"I'll get her to call right after she's finished with her patient."

"Fine." Kia hung up the phone without another word. She sank back in the chair and waited, trying to hang on to the miniscule trace of hope she still had, but it wasn't much. Her breasts ached in her too-tight bra. She unzipped her jeans and placed her palms on the warm skin at the base of her tummy. Was something happening in here? Her stomach was flat, but she did feel different. Was she just imagining it or could she actually sense a tiny life growing inside her?

The ringing of the phone made her jump. Pulling up her zipper with one hand, she grabbed the receiver with the other. She felt the pounding in her chest begin again.

"Hello?"

"Kia."

Kia recognized the male voice. "Yeah, it's me." She knew exactly why Derek was calling.

"Well?"

She shook her head. He was certainly being frugal with words today. "I'm waiting for the doctor to call. I thought you might be her."

"Call me as soon as you hear."

"I will."

The moment Kia hung up it rang again. "Hello?"

"Kia?" This time it was a female voice.

"Yeah, it's me. Dr. Miyata?"

"Yes, hello, Kia. I've got the results of your pregnancy test."

"Uh-huh." She took a deep breath.

"Are you ready?"

"Yeah." She exhaled.

"It was positive."

"Positive? That means …"

"You're pregnant."

Positive. As the truth of it swept over her she felt her stomach heave. Dropping the phone, she ran to the bathroom.

～

Jan. 11

I remember …

— knowing … that he was in the room, and becoming aware, somehow, that he was watching me, like a cat watches its prey. I could feel it. My skin prickled with it.

I remember …

— wondering … why me? I'm not one of his kind, one of the 'beautiful' people, the cool ones.

I remember …

— daring … finally, to look back. Our eyes met and held fast across that crowded, noisy kitchen. He smiled, just a little. My stomach flipped. Did I smile back?

I remember …

— watching … as he crossed the room. He came straight to me. We talked, but the words were not important. Something

had happened. It was like there was only the two of us there, like we were in a bubble of our own, or perhaps a force field surrounded us, one that no one else could enter. It was hypnotic. I knew that the party was going on all around us, yet we were absolutely alone. I was drawn into him, his breathing, his heat, his eyes. It felt like he was looking deep inside me.

I remember ...

– aching ... to be with him. Craving him, from then on. And he seemed to crave me. I couldn't believe that Derek Klassen, THE Derek Klassen, liked me! I became one of THEM.

I can't believe I just wrote that. Is that what it was all about? I am so lame.

From: Kia <hazelnut@hotmail.com>
To: Justin <justintime@yahoo.com>
Date: Jan. 11
Subject: Re: all ears

hey justin, i'm ready to talk. u sure u want to listen? does anyone else read your e-mail?

kia
and T.O.Y. means????

From: Justin <justintime@yahoo.com>
To: Kia <hazelnut@hotmail.com>
Date: Jan. 11
Subject: pour your heart out

kia,
no one else reads my mail. how about yours? would u rather we met in person, or talked on the phone?

T.O.Y. = thinking of you
justin

From: Kia <hazelnut@hotmail.com>
To: Justin <justintime@yahoo.com>
Date: Jan. 11
Subject: Re: pour your heart out

justin,

it's ok. my parents respect my privacy. they think they're the perfect parents, remember? lol.

so here it goes. (i'm taking a deep breath here.)

i'm an idiot.
i hate myself and ...
i'm pregnant.
there, I said it. funny thing tho, i don't feel any better yet.

kia (IBK)

From: Justin <justintime@yahoo.com>
To: Kia <hazelnut@hotmail.com>
Date: Jan. 11
Subject: no more put-downs!!

ok, you're pregnant. it happens. you're in shock, i understand, but you're not a bad person and u're not a stupid
person. i don't want 2 hear anymore of that kind of crap, ok?
u're just pregnant. so, give me some more details. who's the
guy? u don't have 2 answer that but tell me this — is he there
for u? have u talked 2 a doc, your parents, the rev? i can
borrow a car most evenings. why don't i come over so we
can talk face 2 face or we could go somewhere?

T.O.Y.
justin
IBK? what's that?

From: Kia <hazelnut@hotmail.com>
To: Justin <justintime@yahoo.com>
Date: Jan. 11
Subject: Re: no more put-downs!!

justin,

it's ok. e-mail works — i don't want 2 take any more of your time. the guy's name's not important — he's a jerk. (i figured that out just a little 2 late!!!) i've talked 2 a doctor, had a lab test, it was confirmed. i've got an appointment for counseling the day after tomorrow. i can probably get the "procedure" to "terminate the pregnancy" (that's what they call it) next week. i just want to get it over with. my parents don't know. they're cool, they wouldn't freak or anything, but ... i just don't want them 2 know. they'd be so disappointed in me. i haven't even told my best friend. i'm 2 ashamed of myself. you're the only one I'm telling. lucky u! so, as u can see, everything is taken care of. (so why do i feel so horrible?)

kia
(IBK = Idiot Behind Keyboard)

From: Justin <justintime@yahoo.com>
To: Kia <hazelnut@hotmail.com>
Date: Jan. 11
Subject: I'll be there

kia,

it sounds like u are being responsible. u always did seem older than u are. i'm sorry you're feeling horrible. i want u 2 tell me what day 'the procedure' is being done. i'm going 2 swap days off work if i have 2 so i can come with u, and i won't take no for an answer, unless "he" (the jerk) is going with u and you're comfortable with that. i won't interfere if that's the case. otherwise, i'm there, got it?

are you volunteering at the home tomorrow? will I see you
then?
hugs
justin

From: Kia <hazelnut@hotmail.com>
To: Justin <justintime@yahoo.com>
Date: Jan. 11
Subject: Thank you
i'll b there tomorrow. talk to u then.
kia

～

Kia walked into the sunroom of the seniors' home. It was
hot, stuffy, and the human smells mixed with the sharp
odor of cleaning solutions made her stomach roll. She felt
faint, and quickly pulled her sweater off. There was a dozen
or so seniors sitting in the room, some napping in their
wheelchairs, some staring out the window, and a few sitting in groups. She spotted Justin. He was perched on the
edge of a table, talking to a shriveled old man in a wheelchair. There was a blanket over the man's legs, an oxygen
tank strapped to his chair, and a clear tube running up to
his nose. The old man tilted his head back and gave a
hearty laugh at something Justin said. Kia was amazed
that such a loud sound could come from such a frail body.

Justin spotted Kia and quickly crossed the room and
pulled her into a huge hug. The gesture overwhelmed
her, and she had to wipe her eyes when he let her go.

"I think your gang is waiting in the parlor for you,"
he said, smiling down at her.

She nodded. "You haven't changed the name of that

room yet?" she teased half-heartedly. The smallest things had been irritating her lately. "Couldn't we call it the music room?"

"Call it whatever you like, Kia, as long as you keep playing the piano. Your visit is the highlight of the week for many of our residents."

Kia nodded, feeling slightly guilty that the only reason she kept coming was to earn the community service points that she needed for school.

"How are you feeling?" he asked.

"Lousy."

"Then I'm extra proud of you for coming today. And you're coming to Youth Group this week, right?"

She nodded.

"Okay, then let's go. Time to astound them with your talent." Justin walked her down the corridor and pushed the door to the parlor open. "Ladies and gentleman," he said, stepping into the room and winking at the only man present, "may I present Kia Hazelwood, pianist extraordinaire, returning to Willows for a repeat engagement. Let's show her a true Willows welcome!"

The assembled group of senior citizens clapped, while Kia, blushing, stepped up to the piano. She pulled a book out of her bag, placed it on the piano and pushed up her sleeves. She began to play and quickly became lost in the music. Playing one song after another, she paused only long enough to turn the pages in her book. She didn't make eye contact with any of the seniors, nor did she acknowledge their applause. She was determined to do her job and get out of there. After half an hour she closed her book, quietly thanked the audience and started toward the door, but she felt a hand reach out and grab her arm as she tried to leave. She looked down, appalled to see that the hand grasping her arm was gnarled and misshapen. She looked into the eyes of a woman in a wheelchair, and was startled to see tears glistening in them.

"That was lovely, Kia. You are a fine pianist."

"Thank you." She smiled politely, pulled her arm away and tried again to leave.

"You played with a lot more expression today," the old woman continued.

Kia turned back to her, surprised. "I did?"

"Oh yes. It was like you dug way deeper, discovered the emotion in yourself and expressed it in your perform-ance. You didn't just play the notes."

"Huh."

"And you also chose a more somber selection today," she said, her eyes probing Kia's.

"Really." Kia looked away. "I wasn't aware of that."

"My name's Grace," the old woman said, stretching out her hand to shake Kia's.

Kia hoped Grace didn't see her recoil at the sight of that hand again. She gently held it and allowed Grace to shake hers.

"I used to play the piano too," Grace continued, "though not nearly as well as you."

Kia knew she must have looked surprised, because Grace laughed and carried on.

"My hands didn't always look like this, dear," she said. "In fact, I used to be rather proud of them. I had long slim fingers, much like yours." Her eyes took on a faraway expression.

Justin came into the room at that moment, to Kia's relief. "Ah, I see my two favorite ladies have met," he said, placing his hands on Grace's shoulders.

"Yes, Justin, I was just telling Kia that she played particularly well today."

Justin nodded. "I bet Kia needed a compliment today too."

"It wasn't just an empty compliment, she really did," Grace insisted. "And she created a very melancholy mood. It brought tears to my eyes."

"Good music always makes me cry too," Justin said, smiling gently at Grace. "So, did you two introduce yourselves?"

"We did," Grace answered.

"But did you tell Kia your nickname?"

"Oh Justin, of course not."

Kia watched as Grace's pale cheeks flushed.

"Well, Kia," Justin said, "we call Grace Graceful, just because she is."

Kia couldn't think of a more inappropriate nickname for a woman who looked like she was crippled with arthritis, but she smiled and nodded anyway. Grace was shaking her head at Justin, but she was smiling too.

"I've got to go, Justin," Kia said. "Nice meeting you, Grace. I'll see you next week."

"I'm looking forward to it, Kia. Perhaps by then you'll be feeling better and ready to play some more upbeat music again. Get us dancing in our chairs."

Justin and Grace both laughed at the expression on Kia's face. "Music is like poetry," Justin said. "Through it we glimpse the soul."

So, Kia thought gloomily as she headed out the front door, maybe people really could see what was happening to her.

It was a depressing thought.

⌒

Kia's stomach lurched when she entered the kitchen. The smell of meat cooking was nauseating; the thought of eating meat was worse.

"Hi, hon. How was your day?" Her mom looked up from the onion she was dicing.

"Fine."

"That's it? Fine?"

"Yep. That's about it."

Her mom went back to her onion. "Well then, could you throw a salad together for me while I finish this spaghetti sauce?"

"I suppose." At least her mom wasn't cooking one of her weird Filipino dishes. It was a constant battle. Kia and her sister, Angie, insisted on eating western food, but their mom wanted them to appreciate the customs and food of her "home," a small village outside of Manila where she was raised.

Kia rifled through the fridge, looking for things she could put in a salad. When she removed the lettuce she spotted the dill pickles. *Sandwich Stackers*, the label said. Putting the salad makings beside the sink, she went back to the fridge and pulled out the jar of pickles. She took a fork from the cutlery drawer and stabbed one of the pre-sliced dills. She popped it into her mouth, then speared another one.

"How was the French exam?" her mom asked, glancing up from her chopping again.

"Not bad. I think I did okay."

Her mom nodded. "And your report on *Of Mice and Men*? Did you get it back yet?"

"No, not yet." Kia stabbed another pickle. "Is it okay if Shawna comes over to do homework tonight?"

"Yeah, that's fine. How come I haven't seen Derek lately? Isn't his family back from their Christmas vacation yet?"

"Yeah, they're back. But I'm not seeing him anymore. He's a jerk."

"Oh."

Kia knew by her mom's wide-eyed glance that she wanted to hear more, but she'd never ask, and Kia wasn't going to enlighten her. Kia continued eating pickles, unaware that her mom had suddenly stopped chopping and was watching her.

"Kia, the last time I ate so many pickles at one time was when I was pregnant with you."

The fork froze, mid-stab. Kia retracted it from the jar with a weak smile. She noticed the puzzled expression on her mom's face. "I guess that's why I like them so much." She flushed. "I mean, because you ate so many when you were pregnant with me." She screwed the lid on the jar and put it back in the fridge. She glanced at her mom again, fully expecting to find her still staring, but was relieved to see that she was now pressing garlic cloves into the spaghetti sauce.

week 8/40

~ the trunk is straightening out
~ the elbows bend
~ spontaneous movement begins
~ size of a chicken egg

Jan. 13
Two hearts beating …
Inside of me.
Are they in unison
Or does each have its own rhythm?

❧

"What a lovely surprise to see *you*." Jade, counselor at the Planned Parenthood Center, reached across her desk to grasp Derek's hand after shaking Kia's. "So many teenage girls come alone, or with their mothers."

Jade was a black woman with an enormous, booming presence. Her cropped hair was graying at the temples and she wore flashy, dangling earrings. A thick gold ring pierced an eyebrow, and a dozen or more bracelets tinkled on her arm whenever she moved. Kia liked her immediately.

"I look after my own business," Derek said, dropping into a chair beside Kia.

"That's how you see this?" Jade asked him, her eyebrows arched. "As your *business*?"

"What else is it?"

"Well, let's talk about that." Her deep brown, long-lashed eyes settled on Kia. "You're here because you're pregnant and you want to discuss your options."

"She knows what her options are," Derek interrupted. "She's here because she had to come here to book an appointment for an abortion."

"Is that right, Kia?" Jade asked.

Kia shot Derek a look, but then turned and nodded at Jade. Dr. Miyata had urged her to get a counseling appointment as soon as possible, so she'd phoned the Planned Parenthood Center, the appointment was set, and Derek had reluctantly agreed to drive her.

"Terminating your pregnancy is not your only choice, Kia."

"I know that," Kia answered.

"Can you tell me why you think it is the best option for you?"

Kia glanced at Derek. She was just about to answer when he interrupted again.

"Because she's only sixteen! What other option does she have?"

"Many girls choose not to terminate their pregnancies, Derek. Some of them put their babies up for adoption, and many others keep them."

"Well, they're just stupid!" he spat. "Kia wants to get an abortion and get this over with."

"Okay, Derek," Jade said quietly, "I think I now know exactly what *you* think Kia should do. Now I need to hear Kia's opinion."

Derek slumped back in his chair with an exaggerated

sigh. He stared out the window.

"Kia," Jade continued quietly. "Before you got pregnant yourself, how did you feel about abortion?"

Kia considered the question carefully. "Well, first of all, I never thought it was something I was going to have to face. We used birth control." She glanced at Derek. He pointedly ignored her. "But I was assigned the prochoice stand in a debate we had in my sex education class." She shook her head, remembering. "It was weird. By the time the debate was over, everyone was all emotional, even though we were given our positions."

Jade nodded. "It's a controversial topic."

"But I guess I believe every woman should have a right to decide for herself what to do."

"Okay," Jade nodded. "And Derek tells me you've chosen abortion for yourself. Can you tell me why you feel that is the best choice for you?"

Kia glanced at Derek again and found he was now staring at her. She tried not to let him intimidate her, but it was hard. "I guess," she stammered, "it's like Derek says: I'm too young."

"What's wrong with being a young parent?"

"Well, I want to go to college …"

"You still could."

"But it would be way harder, financially and everything."

"That's true. Any other reason?"

"I still want to party with my friends."

"And you think that if you were a parent you wouldn't be able to do that?"

"That's right."

"Okay, that's valid. Anything else?"

Kia was keenly aware that her answers were sounding pretty lame, if only to her own ears. But she continued. "I don't want to disappoint my parents. That's a biggie."

"They don't know?"

"No."

Jade nodded sympathetically. "So that's why continuing with the pregnancy and choosing adoption isn't a good choice for you?"

"Uh-huh. And anyway, it would be way too hard to give up a baby."

"So," Derek said, looking at his watch. "I'd say those were pretty convincing answers, wouldn't you, Jade?"

Jade ignored Derek. "Anything else, Kia?"

Kia regarded Derek. Inspired by Jade's ability to ignore him, she decided to add one last item to her list. "And when I do have a baby some day, I want to have it with someone who loves me," she said, meeting Derek's startled gaze.

"Sounds like a good plan," he said coolly. Then he turned to Jade. "So, do *you* make her the appointment?"

Jade nodded. "Okay, if you're sure about your decision, Kia, you now have two more choices. You could have the procedure done in a hospital where you would be put under a general anesthetic. In other words, you'd be put right out. You wouldn't remember a thing. Or your second option is to go to a clinic where a local anesthetic is used, and you're awake throughout. This is a little quicker, and the recovery is easier as well."

"The clinic, I think," Kia said. "I've never been put right out before. The thought of it gives me the creeps."

"Okay, then I'm going to give you some pamphlets to read while I go and see about setting up an appointment for you. You have to know exactly what is going to happen, and sign a permission form, indicating that you understand the procedure. Any questions?"

Kia shook her head and began to read the pamphlets.

Jade was back a moment later. "How does January the eighteenth sound?" she asked.

Kia looked up from the paper in her hand. She swallowed hard. "Fine, I guess."

"Are you finding that material a little hard to read?" Jade asked quietly, studying Kia's face.

She nodded. "A little."

Derek cleared his throat impatiently.

"But I'm okay," she added.

Jade handed Kia some more paper. "The directions to the clinic are in here, as well as the permission slip you need to sign. If you have any questions at all, either of you," she added, including Derek, "please don't hesitate to call."

Derek pushed back his chair and stood up. "Finally. C'mon, Kia, let's go."

But Jade blocked the doorway. "Kia, part of the reason for this counseling session was for us to go over birth control methods. For the future."

Kia stood beside Derek. "Not to worry," she said. "I won't be back. Trust me."

"Well then, maybe Derek and I should have a talk."

"Very funny, Jade," he said, trying to get by her.

"I wasn't trying to be funny, Derek," she said, stepping out of the way.

Jan. 16
Is the date of my death already determined?
Like the date for the tiny soul living inside me?
How long will I get to live?
Who decides when it's over for me?

She lay on the narrow table, staring up at the abortionist. His eyes were ice-blue, and his smile mocked her. She'd had the injection, the one that was supposed to be a partial anesthetic, but she couldn't move her tongue, her mouth, her arms or legs. She began to panic.

Suddenly he had a scalpel in his hand and was pulling the gown away from her chest and abdomen.

"What are you doing?!" she wanted to scream. She tried to pull the gown back over herself, but she couldn't move. "I'm here for an abortion."

"You'll never have to worry about getting pregnant again, Kia," the blue-eyed doctor told her, gawking at her naked body. "Not when I'm finished with you. And then everything will be okay. We'll sew you back up and then off you go."

The panic intensified. She shook her head from side to side, but the doctor just stood there, smiling down at her, the scalpel poised above her belly.

"Are you sorry now?" he asked, touching the point to her skin.

"Sorry for what?" she wanted to say, but she couldn't use her mouth. She screamed a silent scream and the knife plunged into her.

Kia woke with a jolt and glanced at the clock on her night table. The scarlet numbers glowed in the pitch-black room. 3:14. Sitting up, she groped for the switch on her reading lamp, knowing the light would help diffuse the images from the nightmare more quickly.

She took a deep, ragged breath and leaned back on her pillow. She'd been having a lot of nightmares, but this was the worst one yet. With a trembling hand, she picked up a pen and opened her journal. She waited until the feeling of panic subsided and then wrote whatever came to mind.

~

Jan. 17
Who is in control of me or of this tiny new life?
Me, or him?
Control—does IT have any?
No, IT depends on me.

If you are not born, do you have a soul?
Can you die?
Is birth or conception the first moment of life?
Tomorrow IT dies.
Will IT forgive me?

~

"So, you've been counseled, you understand your options, and you're here of your own free will?" the doctor at the clinic asked. His voice was flat and the expression on his face was deadpan.

Kia nodded.

"And you understand the procedure?"

Kia met his gaze and held it. "Yeah, you're going to dilate my cervix, go into my uterus and scrape off everything that's in there. Then you're going to use a suction to suck it all out."

The doctor's eyebrows arched involuntarily. "I guess that's one way of putting it."

"And I won't let the sound of the suction freak me out. I've been warned."

The doctor stared at her. "You have signed the consent forms?"

Kia nodded.

"Well then," he shuffled the papers on his desk, "your boyfriend has to wait in the lobby, or he can come back in an hour and a half."

"He's not ..." Kia began, but Justin reached over and took her hand. He squeezed it when she looked up at him. He was smiling and shaking his head slightly, so she didn't finish the sentence.

"That's it, then," the doctor said, standing up. "Kia, you can put on one of the gowns that you'll find through there." He pointed to a door across the room. "A nurse will come and get you shortly and I'll see you in the treatment room."

Treatment room, Kia thought. They do the "procedure" in the "treatment" room. No one wants to talk about what is actually happening here.

She stood and looked up at Justin, who towered above her. The top of her head barely reached his chin, but she probably weighed just as much as him, he was so skinny. He reached down and hugged her again, squeezing tightly. She could feel all his bones through his thin shirt.

"I'll be here," he said. "Sending positive energy your way."

The comment was so typically Justin that she smiled, though it was hard. "Thanks," she answered, then turned and followed the doctor through the back door.

～

Kia reached for a gown from the pile. She shook it out and wondered who had last worn it. Another sixteen-year-old perhaps, sick with remorse? She slipped it on and wrapped her arms around herself. She might as well be wearing nothing for all the warmth it gave. Reaching behind her, she clutched together the gap in the back and then peeked out of the cubicle, wondering what she was supposed to do next. There were two chairs and a couple of *Better Health* magazines on a table. She slipped out of the cubicle and sat down, trying to keep the gap in the back of the gown closed. Picking up a magazine, she flipped through a few pages, then put it down again. She couldn't focus on words or pictures.

She thought of Justin waiting in the lobby and instantly felt a little better just knowing he was there. She closed her eyes and tried to picture his face. It was long and narrow, like his build, and his shoulder-length auburn hair, which grew in fuzzy coils, was pulled back into a ponytail, making his face appear even longer. He wore baggy, multicolored pants that could have passed for pajama bottoms, and shirts and vests straight out of the '70s. He'd proudly admitted that he shopped at second-hand stores. There was always a sparkle in his dark brown eyes, and the corners of his wide mouth turned up, like a pixie's, so he looked perpetually happy.

Kia thought back to the day she'd phoned and told Derek that she didn't want him going to the abortion clinic with her.

"What made you think I was planning to?" he'd asked.

She hadn't answered. He was becoming so predictable.

"Kidding," he'd said. But she hadn't been convinced. "So who *is* going with you, then?" he'd asked suspiciously. Kia had forgotten she'd said she wasn't going to tell anyone else.

"A friend from my church," she'd hedged, not wanting to be too specific. "Don't worry, I didn't mention your name."

She was sure she'd heard relief in the silence that followed. For a moment she'd regretted her decision. Maybe she shouldn't have let him off the hook so easily. She should have made him come with her and then insisted he sit in the lobby and wait. It wouldn't be nearly as bad as what she had to go through, but it would have been something.

But she was relieved to have Justin with her, she decided, looking around at the antiseptic surroundings of the clinic. She needed moral support more than she needed the pleasure of punishing Derek.

"Are you okay, dear?" asked a nurse who'd just appeared from another room.

Kia looked up, startled by the question. The words were kind enough, she noticed, but the tone was sharp and the stubborn set of her jaw matched her voice better than the words.

"Yeah, I guess."

"You're holding your stomach. I thought maybe you were sick."

Kia looked down and noticed that both of her hands were once again resting on her stomach. She'd caught herself assuming this protective position a lot lately. Protective? That was a joke, she thought, considering what she was about to do to the tiny life inside her.

"No." She took her hands off her stomach. "I'm all right." But it was a lie.

"Good. Then follow me. We're going to the treatment room now."

Kia wondered if her knees were going to buckle under her weight when she stood up, and suddenly she did feel queasy.

The nurse led her down a corridor and opened a door at the far end. They entered a large room with a sterile-looking cot in the center. Beside the bed all kinds of surgical equipment lay on a cart. Kia thought it looked like something out of *The X-Files*. The doctor was standing at the back of the room, pulling on latex gloves.

"Climb up," the nurse instructed, "and put your feet in the stirrups."

Kia did as she was told, and stared at the ceiling. Her hands gripped the metal rails at the side of the cot. She forced herself to focus on a small black stain overhead as she fought back tears. Even with the doctor and the nurse in the room, she'd never felt so alone in her life. She began to tremble. The nurse draped a sheet over her and then wrapped a blood-pressure band around her arm. Kia felt the band squeeze, and then release. The nurse jotted something on a clipboard and pushed a thermometer into Kia's mouth. She lifted Kia's wrist, felt for the pulse and then studied her watch. She wrote down the information and pulled the thermometer out of Kia's mouth. Then with the ease that comes from years of practice, she slid a thin needle into the skin on the back of Kia's hand and strung the tubing up to a pole above her head.

Kia heard the doctor approach.

"Everything okay, Kia?" he asked, his voice muffled behind a surgical mask that covered his nose and mouth.

She stared up at him. Here she was, lying on a narrow cot in an abortion clinic, covered only by a thin hospital gown and sheet, with her feet in stirrups, waiting for him to scrape out the little life inside her, and he was asking her if everything was okay? Was he serious?

A little groan escaped her, but he must have taken that for an affirmative answer because she heard him sit on the stool at the foot of the cot and she felt the sheet and gown being lifted away from her legs. He pressed her knees apart, and she heard the tray rattle as he took something off it.

"The first thing I'm going to do is insert this speculum, just like when you have an internal exam," he said. "It will feel cold, but it won't hurt."

It won't hurt, Kia thought. Not this part. But the next part might. She'd been told to expect some discomfort, even with the local anesthetic. And what would the tiny fetus feel when it was being scraped off the side of her uterus? The little baby whose heart was already beating and who was probably a beautiful light tan color, a cross between her skin tone and Derek's. As she felt the cold instrument enter her, she suddenly came to a realization.

"Take it out," she ordered, struggling to sit up. The nurse at her side grabbed her arm and tried to push her back down, but she felt the cold instrument slide back out anyway.

"What's the matter, Kia?" asked the doctor, looking alarmed. "Did that hurt?"

"Let go of me," Kia ordered the nurse. The doctor nodded, and Kia sat up. "I've changed my mind. I can't go through with this." She pulled the gown over her legs and swung them over the side of the cot.

"Kia," the doctor said quietly, placing his hand on her leg so she wouldn't jump up. "You're just nervous. It's a normal reaction. Why don't we give you a little something to help you relax?"

"No." She shook her head. "This is more than nerves. I really have changed my mind. I'm sorry, but I have to leave."

"Listen, young lady," the nurse snapped. "This is not acceptable. You've had the consultation where you were supposed to make a final decision. This appointment has been reserved especially for you. We're not going to welcome you back when you come to your senses."

"I won't be coming back," Kia said. "I'm sure." She pulled the Velcro tab on the blood-pressure band and it fell off her arm. "I'm sorry I let it go this far. But please," she said, pushing the doctor's hand off her leg, "let me go. I need to get out of here."

"Kia," the doctor said after glancing sharply at the

nurse. "The procedure will be over in twenty minutes and then you can get on with your life. This will become just a dim memory. Pregnancy, on the other hand, is another seven months long, childbirth can be difficult and painful, and then you'll have to decide what to do with the child, and you're really not much more than a child yourself." He shook his head. "I think you're letting your emotions influence your common sense."

Kia knew she had to sound rational. "I know this is the right thing for a lot of girls," she said, then cleared her throat, trying to suppress the quiver she heard there, "but I just realized it's not right for me. I'm sorry I didn't see that before," she continued, looking the nurse right in the eye.

The doctor stood up, defeated. "Take the IV out," he instructed.

The nurse tore the tape off Kia's hand and pulled out the needle. Then, with as much dignity as she could muster, Kia climbed off the stretcher, reached around and tugged the back of the gown together again and walked toward the door. Without glancing back she returned to the cubicle, quickly changed into her clothes and found her way back to the waiting room and Justin.

"Justin."

He looked up sharply. "Kia, what are you doing here?"

"I changed my mind." Once again she felt her voice catching in her throat. "Let's go. Quick."

He jumped up, putting his arm around her shoulder, and guided her through the door, into the rain. It was a short walk to the car, but they were both soaked by the time they reached it. He opened the passenger door and waited while she got in. Then he climbed into the driver's seat and turned to look at her.

"Are you okay, Kia?"

"I'm going to be now." She nodded, thinking about it. For the first time in weeks, she felt in control of her own life.

He studied her, then pulled off his wire-rimmed glasses, dried them on his shirt and put them back on. He started the car and pulled out into the traffic. "We'll go somewhere quiet to talk, okay?"

"Thanks."

Neither of them said a word until Justin pulled into a driveway. "This is my parents' house," he said, adding sheepishly, "I still live at home."

"So do I."

"Yeah, but I'm a bit older than you, and I've been out of school for years. Anyway, no one's home."

Kia nodded and climbed out of the car.

After hanging their coats on hooks beside the door, Justin plugged the kettle in to make tea. Kia sank into a chair in the kitchen. Looking around, she decided the room looked a lot like Justin himself—kind of funky, a bit cluttered and unconventional, but cheerful and warm. He sat down across the table from her while he waited for the water to boil.

"I take it you didn't have the abortion," he said, his voice gentle.

"No. I was in the treatment room, he was just about to begin, and then ..." Her voice trailed off.

"And then?"

"Oh, God, it was awful." Kia covered her face with her hands.

Justin waited quietly.

"I suddenly really understood, for the first time," she said, dropping her hands, "what was going to happen—what I had consented to."

"You had the counseling session. Weren't your options explained to you?"

"Yeah, they were, but I guess they didn't sink in. Or maybe I just didn't allow myself to think it through." She struggled to explain it. "I was with Derek and he was so sure about what we had to do that I just went along with it, not ever stopping to think that he might not be right." Kia recalled her journal entries. "Well, I guess I was thinking about it, but I didn't do anything about it. It was easier to let someone else make the decision."

Justin nodded.

"But lying there I realized that I don't want anything bad to happen to this baby." She rubbed her face. She was so tired. "Derek's going to be so ticked."

"Don't worry about him."

"Thanks, Justin." She smiled at him, her eyes shining. "I don't know what I would have done without you today."

"You would have been fine."

She looked away. "Thanks for pretending to be my boyfriend, too."

"Any time."

They sat quietly for a minute, listening to the rain.

"In a way," she continued, "Derek was right. It could have been all over with by now, no one would have found out, and my life wouldn't be ruined ..."

"Ruined?"

"Yeah, like the doctor said, it would just become a faded memory in time."

"But now you think you've chosen to ruin your life?"

The kettle whistled. Justin got up to make the tea.

"Now I'm going to have a baby." Kia placed both hands on her stomach and felt the warmth of her palms travel through her shirt and onto her skin. She wondered if the fetus could feel it too. "I'm going to have to tell everyone—my parents, my friends ... everyone. And I'm going to get big and fat, and then I have to go through childbirth." She turned to Justin. "Maybe I haven't ruined my life, but it's going to mess it up for a long time. Oh man," she sighed. "What have I done?"

Justin put a steaming mug on the table in front of her and returned to his chair.

"But you know," she said, taking a sip of her tea, "I did the right thing for me. And," she added, her hands resting on her stomach again, her palms almost hugging it, "I did the right thing for this little guy."

"Little guy?" Justin asked.

"You know what I mean," she answered. Then she grinned, thinking of the photos she'd seen during the sexuality classes at Youth Group. "Little Peanut. That's what I'll call it. At eight weeks they look almost like a peanut."

Justin came over and placed one hand on her shoulder and one on her stomach. "Hey, Peanut," he said. "Pleased to meet you."

His touch made Kia feel awkward, even though she knew he was trying to set her at ease. The heat from his hand on her skin was an unpleasant reminder of Derek.

"Listen," she said, finding an excuse to change the subject. "I think it's finally stopped raining." The room was quickly becoming brighter. Justin left her side and walked over to the window, pulling back the sheer curtains. "You're right," he said. "And the sun is trying to come out. And look who's here."

Kia joined him at the window and peered out toward the driveway. "Who?"

Justin went to the kitchen cupboard for a cup and rejoined Kia at the window. "Not outside," he said. "Here." He pointed at a hairy black spider walking along the window ledge.

"Oh, gross!" Kia said, stepping back.

"He's not gross, he's beautiful." Justin watched as it scurried away from them. "He's an old guy to have gotten this big." With one swift motion he placed the cup over the spider and slid a sheet of paper underneath it. With the spider trapped inside, he slipped out the door, squatted down and gently released it outside. "There you go, old fellow." He stood up and stretched. "Hey, would you look at that?" he said, standing on the porch.

"What?" Cautiously, Kia came up beside him, fully expecting to see another spider.

"There's a rainbow. Or half a rainbow, anyway."

"Cool. I haven't seen one in ages."

"Did you know the rainbow is a universal sign of hope?"

Kia nodded. It was fitting. Right now she was feeling more hopeful than she had in weeks.

They were on their second pot of tea when Justin finally asked Kia when she thought she'd break the news to her parents.

"I don't know," she answered. "I suppose I could tell them right away, but they might try to get me to reconsider the abortion thing again. If I wait until the fourth month they won't be as likely to suggest it."

Justin nodded thoughtfully. "Why don't you talk to Reverend Petrenko about it? He's cool, and he might suggest the best way to go about talking to them.

"Yeah, well, he might push abortion too."

"No, that's not his style. He doesn't push his views on anyone. He'll listen to what you have to say and figure out how to help."

Kia shrugged. "Okay. If you think it's important."

"Yeah, I do. I'll set up the meeting, if you like."

"Will you come with me?"

"Count on it."

"Thanks." Kia looked away, embarrassed. "Aren't you afraid he might think you're the father?"

Justin didn't respond at first. When she glanced back at him, an odd expression had crossed his face, an expression that Kia couldn't quite read. "He won't think that, and besides, I try not to worry about what people think anymore, Kia. And you know," he added, "it would be a good thing for you to get over too. Especially now."

Kia sensed he was telling her something more, but she didn't ask.

"So, are you ready to go home?"

"Yeah, I am. Thanks." She took her coat from him. "You know, I've managed to get through the last few weeks without actually lying to my parents about anything. I've just avoided the issue of what I've been up to. But I sure hope nobody asks me where I was today. I don't think I'd be able to lie with a straight face."

"They'll just assume you were at school, won't they?"

"Yeah, unless the school phoned to report that I was absent."

"Well, there was that rainbow. I think you'll be lucky today."

"It was only half a rainbow."

Justin held the door for her. "I'd say you need a little attitude adjustment," he said as she passed by him. "You're seeing a half-empty glass where you should be seeing a half-full one."

Kia smiled. "Funny you should mention attitude," she said. "My parents are always bringing it up too. They say I have way too much."

Justin laughed, and the sound of it improved her mood even more than the tea and conversation had. She'd accepted that she was going to have a baby. Now, if only she could get everyone else to accept it.

week 10/40

~ eyelids cover eyes
~ toes and upper lip have formed
~ external ears are complete
~ plum-sized

Jan. 24

We never talked much. It seemed like we didn't need words. I'd never experienced anything like it before. We were magnets, drawn to each other, an unstoppable force. Just being together was enough.

Or so I thought.

It seems I thought a lot of things ... like our feelings for each other were mutual ...

I remember that day so clearly. It was right before he was leaving to go on holidays with his family. We were alone. I couldn't bear the thought of being apart. It was a physical pain. He lit some candles and poured us some wine that he'd taken from his parents. We toasted each other, and had a second glass.

That night the soft kisses and gentle stroking just weren't enough. We undressed each other slowly, and he touched me in that special way he has and I wanted him so badly ...

I knew I should stop before it went too far. But I didn't. I was no longer in the real world. It was like he had ignited a fire in me and I couldn't (wouldn't?) put it out. What could go wrong when it felt so good?

Only everything.

～

"So Kia, Justin tells me you're pregnant."

Kia glanced at Justin. She nodded. They were in the Reverend's office at the church.

"And you're not in a committed relationship?"

"No." Kia shook her head and looked away. "That's why I almost had an abortion, but I couldn't go through with it."

The Reverend had to lean forward to hear her. "No? Why couldn't you do it?"

She shrugged. "I guess I was trying to believe it was the only option for me, but at the last minute I didn't want to do it." She placed a hand on her stomach. "I'd already connected with my baby."

Reverend Petrenko nodded and studied her. "That was a brave decision. It's not easy being a pregnant teen in our society."

"You're telling me," Kia replied. She shifted uncomfortably in her chair.

"Character-building stuff," Justin said, putting his arm over the back of her chair. "I know she can handle it," he added, smiling down at her.

"Society is so hypocritical, isn't it?" The Reverend sat back in his chair, his hands clasped behind his head. "Sexual references are everywhere," he mused. "You can't walk by a newsstand or even watch prime-time TV without being inundated with them. Yet we still expect teens to choose abstinence." He shook his head and scratched his neat black beard thoughtfully. "Our own Sex Education course encourages abstinence," he continued, "but also teaches that sexuality is a wonderful human experience. How can we expect teens to choose to abstain when these powerful messages are everywhere, yet when a girl gets pregnant ..."

The unfinished sentence hung in the air. Kia wondered if he'd said more than he'd meant to.

"Anyway," he said, leaning forward again, "you are pregnant, you've considered your options, and you've chosen to have the baby. Where do we go from here?"

"I don't know." Kia shrugged and picked at her nail polish.

"Justin tells me you haven't told your parents yet."

"No."

"Would you like me to be with you when you do?"

Kia hesitated, considering the offer, then shook her head. "Thanks, but that's okay. I can do it."

He nodded. "So then what?" he asked gently. "Once they've accepted that you're having a baby, they'll want to know what you plan to do with it."

"I know."

"Have you given it any thought?" His deep voice was softer than usual.

Kia shook her head. She felt her hands go to her stomach again.

"Are you thinking of asking your parents to help you raise it?"

"No." She answered quickly. "Mom's finally back at school working on her Ph.D. She wouldn't want to look after another baby. Neither would Dad."

"Are you thinking of raising it on your own, then?"

Kia just shrugged again.

"That would certainly be a challenge for a girl your age. Social assistance helps, but being a single teen parent takes a lot of courage, not to mention work, and it makes getting an education more difficult and more expensive. Your whole future is affected."

Kia didn't answer. She chewed nervously at a fingernail.

There was a long pause. "One thing I can do as your minister," he suggested finally, "is connect you with a social worker who can help you select good parents to adopt your child."

"Yeah?" Kia asked, without enthusiasm.

"That's right. You don't have to hand the child over to strangers anymore. You can choose couples on the wait list who you think share the same values as you do, and then interview as many as it takes to find the right ones."

Kia nodded but didn't look up.

"And as you know," he continued, warming to his subject, "there are many childless couples who are anxious to adopt a baby. Mature couples who are economically stable and ready for the responsibility of a child ..."

"Hang on," Justin interrupted after studying Kia's face. "I think Kia needs to deal with one thing at a time," he said. "First she needs to tell her parents. She can think about this stuff later."

"You're right, Justin," the Reverend said. "I apologize. I'm getting ahead of myself again. Just one of my many bad habits. But Kia, I'm glad you came by to talk to me. You'll come and see me any time, right? Especially if the going gets rough?"

Kia nodded absent-mindedly. She was studying a poster hanging on one of the walls in the office. It showed a blue car, the image blurred as it raced toward a hairpin turn on a deserted road. *CHANGE* was written across the top. Underneath the picture it stated: A *bend in the road is not the end of the road ... unless you fail to make the turn.*

"Are you coming, Kia?"

She blinked. Justin was holding open the door for her and she could hear him jingling his car keys. She stood up and shook the minister's extended hand, put thoughts of the poster aside and followed Justin out to his car.

From: Kia <hazelnut@hotmail.com>
To: Justin <justintime@yahoo.com>
Date: Jan. 25
Subject: hairpin turns

hey justin, u know that poster inside the rev's office? the one about the bend in the road? well, i've been thinking. if the road is life, and for me, the bend was getting pregnant, i'm wondering if i made the right turn. u know? will having this baby change the direction of my life, or will it just be a detour?

C U
K

From: Justin <justintime@yahoo.com>
To: Kia <hazelnut@hotmail.com>
Date: Jan. 25
Subject: Re: hairpin turns

hey kia, interesting question. you're quite the philosopher. the rev explained 2 me once that part of his job is helping people navigate through the changes in their lives. that's why he likes that poster.

it seems 2 me that the answer for u depends on what u do with the baby. it'll be a change—a permanent change—if u keep it. it will be a detour if u put it up for adoption. life is a series of changes, really, one after another, but with this decision you'll have to decide how big of a change u want to make.

justin
ps. u know, most of us stay on the same road, day after day, but forced detours can help us see places and things that were just barely hidden from view before. keep your eyes open. u never know what u may discover!

ttfn
J.

~ fingernails are appearing
~ mouth opens and closes
~ signs of baby's sex are beginning to appear
~ lime sized

Feb. 1
I came to a bend in the road. I took the turn.
My life is not ruined. It's only changed.

From: Justin <justintime@yahoo.com>
To: Kia <hazelnut@hotmail.com>
Date: Feb. 2
Subject: T.O.Y
hey kia. have you made that appointment with the doc?
can i give u a ride?

J

From: Kia <hazelnut@hotmail.com>
To: Justin <justintime@yahoo.com>
Date: Feb. 2
Subject: Re: T.O.Y.
hi justin. i made the app. but i'll take the bus. i need to know
how 2 get there when you're not around. thanks anyway.
i'm going back to dr. miyata. she's cool.

k

From: Justin <justintime@yahoo.com>
To: Kia <hazelnut@hotmail.com>
Date: Feb. 2
Subject: Bussing it

ok but give the peanut a pat for me. tell him to behave.

justin
ps. when are u going to have the talk with your folks?

From: Kia <hazelnut@hotmail.com>
To: Justin <justintime@yahoo.com>
Date: Feb. 2
Subject: he's a she!

justin, u mean HER. i'm sure of it. so i'll give "her" your message. lol. and the talk? soon (maybe). you'll be the first 2 know. honest.

C U L8R
k

"So, you've decided to go through with the pregnancy." Dr. Miyata sat back in her chair and looked across the desk at Kia.

Kia nodded.

"How does your boyfriend feel about that?"

Kia quickly looked down at her hands. "He's not my boyfriend. And he doesn't know," she added quietly.

The doctor's eyebrows shot up and she tilted her head. "No?"

"No."

"But he is the father of this child?"

"Yeah."

"Then don't you think he should know?"

"Uh-huh. I'll tell him. I just haven't got around to it."

"And your parents?"

Kia sighed. This was beginning to feel like an interrogation. "I'm going to tell them soon too."

"How soon?"

"I thought I'd wait until it was too late for an abortion. Then they wouldn't try to make me change my mind."

"Some abortions are done much later than twelve weeks. But you're right, the first trimester is preferable. Are you afraid of their reaction?"

Kia paused before she answered. "It's not that I'm afraid. It's just that they're going to be so stunned. I've been the perfect first-born daughter for a long time."

"That's a tough role to play, all right." The doctor smiled. "I'm surprised you know about birth order and behavior patterns and those kinds of things."

"I know a lot of stuff."

"I'm beginning to realize that. But do you know much about pregnancy?"

"No, not a whole lot. I've seen pictures of fetuses at different stages of development."

The doctor nodded. "Nine months may seem like a long time, but it is miraculous that a complex human being can develop in such a short time."

Kia sat quietly, both arms wrapped around her stomach.

"We'll need to sign you up for prenatal classes. You'll want to find someone to go with you."

"Well, I'm not taking Derek, and I'd feel kind of

stupid bringing my mom when all the others will be married couples." Kia slumped lower in her chair.

"You'll be surprised at the couples you'll find in these classes, Kia. Families aren't what they used to be. Perhaps you have a friend that would go with you? Someone who'd be willing to stick by you right up until the birth?"

Kia's first thought was of Shawna. But then she thought of Justin. Would he be willing to do that for her, or would that be pushing the limits of their friendship?

"I know of one adopting family who went through the prenatal classes with the teen who was carrying their child."

Kia studied the doctor's face. Why was everyone assuming she'd decided on adoption?

"I need to see you once a month until the thirtieth week," the doctor continued. "Then I'll see you twice monthly. Toward the end I'd like to see you each week. In the meantime, I want you to have an ultrasound test so we can determine the exact age the baby is now. Any questions?"

Kia thought for a moment. "Do you think I made the right choice?"

The doctor paused, but only for a moment. "Only you can answer that, Kia. The right choice is different for everyone. It all depends on your circumstances and your values."

Kia nodded. It was the answer she'd expected. "Will you deliver my baby?"

"I sure will. Even if you require a Caesarean section I'll be in the operating room assisting. Okay?"

"Thanks. And I don't need that ultrasound. I know exactly what day the baby was conceived. I'm eleven weeks pregnant."

"That may be so, Kia. But the ultrasound will give us other information too, like if it is a single baby or twins." She jotted something else on a fresh sheet of paper and handed it to Kia. "Here are the phone numbers you need to set up the exam and to register for prenatal classes. Make the calls as soon as you can, okay?"

Kia nodded.

"Good. Now off we go to the examining room to check you over."

Kia used her elbow to clear the steam off the bus window. She looked out at the gray day. The physical exam had been painless. The doctor had measured her stomach, which was still flat, taken her blood pressure and listened for the baby's heartbeat, which she said she couldn't yet detect. It would be beating, the doctor had said, but there were too many other sounds drowning it out. In another month it would be strong enough to be heard clearly. Then she'd given Kia a package of information about pregnancy to read. "It's especially important for you to take care of yourself," the doctor had said, "because you're so young, and still growing yourself. We don't want your health to suffer and we want to create as healthy an environment for the baby as we can." Kia had shoved the information into her backpack.

As the bus shuddered to a stop, Kia glanced at her watch. With any luck, she'd beat her parents home and would have time to make the phone calls. Her sister, Angie, would still be at after-school care ...

Angie. Kia felt a pang of guilt. Last night at dinner

nine-year-old Angie had looked up at her with those big, trusting brown eyes and pointed out that Kia hadn't picked her up from her daycare in ages, since before Christmas. As if from a great distance, Kia had heard herself promising that she'd pick her up the very next day, saying they'd hang out together, just the two of them, just like they used to do. She'd said it, knowing full well that she had a doctor's appointment. What had she been trying to prove? That she was still the perfect big sister? The word "denial" floated fuzzily to the surface of Kia's consciousness, but she pushed it back down.

She decided to stop by right now and collect Angie, even though it was almost time for their parents to arrive home.

Kia stepped off the bus and began the short walk to the daycare. How would Angie take the news about the baby? She felt her stomach flip. She would be shocked. Or disgusted. Probably both. Her one night of sex with Derek was going to affect more lives than she would ever have thought possible.

Kia spotted her mom's car in the driveway of the daycare the moment she turned onto the street. She stopped and considered leaving so she wouldn't have to explain where she'd come from, but before she could, her mom and Angie emerged from the house. Her little sister bounced down the front steps, spotted Kia and waved. "Hey Ki!" she called out. "Perfect timing. Now we can both get a ride."

Her mom looked up, surprised. "Where did you come from, honey?"

"I just got off the bus. I came to pick up Angie. How

come you're here so early?"

"My last class got out early." She studied Kia, puzzled. "Where did you go on the bus?"

Kia felt her face flush. She was a lousy liar. With a sudden change of heart she decided not to lie. "I had a doctor's appointment."

"You did?"

"Uh-huh."

Kia watched her mom's face change as a whole range of emotions flashed across it.

"Don't worry, Mom. I'm okay. I'll tell you about it later."

"Oh." Her mom looked at her with a blank expression and then climbed into the car. She glanced at Angie, and then a look of realization crossed her face. "Ohhh," she said again.

"You can tell me," Angie said, accurately reading her mother's reaction. "I'm not a little kid. I keep telling you, I'm too old for that stupid daycare too. They're all babies there. I have nothing to do."

Kia felt herself flinch at the word "babies."

"One more year, Angie," her mom said patiently. "That's all."

They rode home in silence, Angie already forgetting about the doctor's appointment. Kia swallowed. The ever-present nausea had intensified. She'd committed herself. Tonight was the night.

When she got home, she went straight to her room, shut the door behind her and pulled out her journal.

Feb. 5
I hate myself.
I don't deserve this family.
Maybe I'll wake up and find this was all just a bad dream.
I wish.

⁓

Angie had gone to a movie with a friend, so Kia was alone in the house with her parents. She found them both in the family room, her dad reading the paper and her mom leafing through a textbook.

"So, you said you went to see the doctor today, Kia?" her mom asked in a deliberately casual voice, but Kia noticed the twitching foot. "Is everything okay?" She closed her book and regarded Kia with her dark, almond-shaped eyes.

Kia plunked herself into a chair and faced them. She wondered if they could hear the racket her heart was making in her chest. "I was at the doctor's, but not Dr. Eldridge. I've found a new one. Her name is Dr. Miyata."

"What's wrong with Dr. Eldridge?" asked her mom.

"Nothing." It came out defensive, slightly angry, despite her attempt to remain calm.

"Okay," her father said, nodding, encouraging her to go on, but Kia could see the reddish flush that was creeping up his neck. His bright blue eyes stared back from under thick, graying eyebrows.

Kia drew in a deep breath. This was the moment. She felt her own face burning. "I'm about eleven weeks pregnant."

Her father's skin turned completely crimson, and the textbook on her mother's lap dropped unnoticed to the floor.

"You're sure?" her father asked quietly.

"Yes. I've been tested." Kia found she couldn't meet his eyes.

"I didn't know you were sexually active." Kia's mom's face looked pale in contrast to her dad's.

Kia rolled her eyes. Sexually active made it sound like she was doing it all the time. "I'm not, Mom. I did it once. That's it."

Her parents continued to stare at her.

"I don't blame you if you don't believe me about the just once part," she said, uncomfortable with the silence. "I find it hard to believe too. And I guess it doesn't matter whether it was once or a hundred times. We used birth control but I got pregnant and now I have to deal with it."

"Derek?" her dad asked.

"Yeah." Kia nodded, looking away. "That's the worst part. I just figured out he's a complete jerk."

The icy silence returned.

"I knew a couple weeks ago," she said, rambling on just to break the absolute quiet in the room. "I didn't want to hurt you, and Derek insisted, so I went to a clinic to have an abortion. I got as far as the procedure room before I changed my mind."

"Changed your mind?" her dad asked, as if that wasn't clear enough.

"Yeah. Changed my mind. Decided I was not going through with it."

"Why not?" he asked.

"Because."

"Because?"

"Yeah. It didn't feel right."

"It didn't feel right."

"That's what I said."

"So you're not going to have an abortion?" he asked.

"No, I'm not." Kia wondered what it was about the words "not going through with it" that he didn't understand.

"The pickles …" her mom said.

Kia's dad looked at his wife, puzzled. She just shook her head.

"Derek doesn't know I haven't had the abortion." Kia clenched her fists, her nails digging into her palms. "He's going to be really ticked. But I don't care. He was a huge mistake and it's none of his business what I do."

Her parents continued to stare mutely, so she continued. "I've talked to Reverend Petrenko about it. And Justin Reid knows too. He came to the abortion clinic with me."

"You told all of them but you didn't tell us?" her mom asked quietly.

Kia cleared her throat. "I didn't want to hurt you," she said. "If I'd had the abortion you'd never have known, and you would have gone on thinking I was the perfect daughter."

"We know you're not the perfect daughter, Kia," her dad said defensively. "Nobody's perfect, and that includes you."

"I always felt like I had to be."

"Oh." Her parents glanced at each other.

"So if you're not going to have an abortion," her dad continued, clearing his throat, "that means you plan to have a baby." He seemed to have pulled himself together more quickly than her mom.

"Yeah. I am. And I was thinking about that this afternoon. I know it's going to be embarrassing for you and Mom and really hard on Angie. If you'd like me to go away for awhile ..."

"Go away?" Her father frowned, running his hand across the remaining gray bristles on the top of his head. "Where would you go?"

"I could go stay with ... I don't know. We must know someone who would take me in until after the baby is born."

"I'm sure we could think of someone," he said. "But," he looked at his wife, "I don't want you to go away."

Kia's mom closed her eyes and shook her head. Kia sensed she was in some kind of shock. "Unless you want to," she said quietly.

"No. I'm kinda getting used to the idea of being pregnant."

They sat quietly for another minute. Then her father got up and began to pace in front of the fireplace. He came to a halt and looked down at her.

She knew exactly what he was going to say.

"Are you sure you won't reconsider?"

Kia shook her head and folded her arms around her stomach. She glanced at her mom, unnerved by her silence. Her hands were clenched in her lap and her head was bent forward. She looked like she was praying.

"It would be the best thing for everyone," her dad continued.

"Not for the baby."

"You were our baby, Kia," he argued. "And we want what's best for you. If you have an abortion you'll be able to get on with your life again. We can forget this ever happened."

Kia shook her head. She looked to her mom for support, but she couldn't see her face.

"Give it some more thought," her dad encouraged, his voice sounding hoarse. "I think you're making a big mistake."

"It seems so obvious to you, doesn't it, Dad?" Kia's own voice was trembling. "Just get rid of it. Out of sight, out of mind." Kia folded her arms across her chest. "I thought that was the answer too, but I was wrong." She glanced at her mom again, puzzled by her silence. She saw her dad look at his wife too, then sink back on the couch. "You know," she continued, "I was going to wait a few more weeks before I told you about the baby just to avoid this conversation."

Her mom finally looked up, then turned to look at Kia's father. Their eyes met. Kia wondered what message had passed between them. Her father cleared his throat again. "You seem to have thought this through."

"I have."

He slumped a little deeper into the couch. "So what happens after the baby is born?"

"I don't know yet." She shook her head. "Reverend Petrenko says he can hook me up with couples waiting to adopt. If I want, I can choose the baby's parents."

Kia looked into her mom's eyes. Kia had to look away, and for a moment she wished she'd gone through with the abortion.

"If you want?" her dad asked. He sat up suddenly. He leaned toward her, frowning. "What does that mean exactly?"

Kia was surprised to hear the impatience in his voice. This had pushed even his tolerance, and it was usually high.

"I just don't know yet," Kia said. "Give me some time."

He slammed his fist on the coffee table, making Kia jump at the unexpected force of it. "You better get a grip, girl," he said, his voice husky. "I can understand that you won't have an abortion. But don't plan to raise this child. I won't support that decision."

Kia looked at her mom and nodded. They'd made themselves perfectly clear. The battle lines were drawn. Kia just had to decide whether she was in the fight.

∽

Feb. 6
I have redefined myself.
No longer the perfect child.
I feel release.

∽

From: Kia <hazelnut@hotmail.com>
To: Justin <justintime@yahoo.com>
Date: Feb. 7
Subject: the talk

hi justin. i did it, told my parents 'the news'. i might as well
have taken a knife and plunged it through their hearts. i
think if i'd confessed to being a drug addict or a hooker it
wouldn't have hurt them more. they didn't yell or scream. i
wish they had. then i wouldn't feel so alien on those days
when i flip out.

k

From: Justin <justintime@yahoo.com>
To: Kia <hazelnut@hotmail.com>
Date: Feb. 7
Subject: Re: the talk

hi kia & peanut,
i'm proud of you kia. that is one of the hardest things u'll
ever have to do, and i bet u did it with style. once they're
over the shock it will get easier. imagine how u'd feel if
they'd given u some tuff stuff, like they were separating or
something. u'd feel devastated & angry, but as u grew used
to it u'd accept it. your parents are doing the same thing.
they don't love u any less. they just have to get used 2 the
new u. give them time.

T.O.Y.
justin

From: Kia <hazelnut@hotmail.com>
To: Justin <justintime@yahoo.com>
Date: Feb. 7
Subject: A request

hi justin.
how did you get so wise? those old people u work with are
lucky, but i think maybe you'd make a good minister. did
you ever think of that? or a shrink or something.

i have a question to ask u, but u have to promise to say no
if u don't want 2 do it. promise? cross your heart? ok. i
need someone 2 go 2 prenatal classes with me. i'll ask
shawna if you're not into it. really. truly. it's not a problem.

k

From: Justin <justintime@yahoo.com>
To: Kia <hazelnut@hotmail.com>
Date: Feb. 7
Subject: Re: a request

hi kia and little peanut.
i'd love 2 go 2 prenatal classes with u. it may be the only
chance i'll ever get. is it ok if i call myself uncle even if i'm
only a pretend one?

and no, i've never considered being a minister or psychia-
trist. lol. can u see me trying 2 act proper, with a suit and
tie? or even a jacket and lace-up shoes? i like my old
people. so many of them are lonely and it's my personal
goal to make each one of them laugh every day, or at least
smile. i don't think I've failed yet. a perfect record. how's
that for job success?

hugs,
uncle justin (it has a nice ring 2 it, don't u think?)

From: Kia <hazelnut@hotmail.com>
To: Justin <justintime@yahoo.com>
Date: Feb. 7
Subject: uncle justin

I love it!! :-)

i'm going to tell angie and shawna about the peanut this
weekend. wish me luck. and then i think it's time to tell the

youth group. so bring some ice packs in case anyone
faints.

k & p

From: Justin <justintime@yahoo.com>
To: Kia <hazelnut@hotmail.com>
Date: Feb. 7
Subject: Fingers and toes are crossed
hi kia & peanut,
it will be a historical moment in the youth group's check-in.
expect a group hug. and good luck with angie and
shawna. they luv u. they'll accept what u're doing.

ttfn
uncle justin

From: Kia <hazelnut@hotmail.com>
To: Justin <justintime@yahoo.com>
Date: Feb. 7
Subject: Sex!
justin,
it's not whether they'll accept what i'm doing that bothers
me. it's whether they'll accept what i've done. shawna will.
angie will think it's gross. (right now I think it's gross too. i
may be off sex for the rest of my life. lol)

k & p

From: Justin <justintime@yahoo.com>
To: Kia <hazelnut@hotmail.com>
Date: Feb. 7
Subject: Re: Sex!
kia,

catchy subject! i did lol. and i don't think u need 2 worry about being off sex for the rest of your life. the human sex drive is an impressive thing.

so when do prenatal classes start?

hugs to u both
uncle justin

From: Kia <hazelnut@hotmail.com>
To: Justin <justintime@yahoo.com>
Date: Feb. 7
Subject: Prenatal

hi justin,
you're right about the sex drive thing. perhaps we need a pill to turn it off until we're old enough 2 "handle the responsibility" as they say. (and i'd pay someone to give derek an overdose. ha ha.)

prenatal classes start in 2 weeks. the first ones are mostly about nutrition and exercise. then they start up again in the spring and we learn about birth and babies.

c ya mon.
k & p

Shawna wrapped the elastic around the bottom of the French braid. "There," she said, standing back and assessing her handiwork. "Perfecto moi."

"Perfecto moi? Stick to Russian, Shawn." Kia twisted her neck to see the back of her head in the mirror. "Not bad. Next week it's cornrows. You'd better start practicing on one of your old Barbie dolls."

Shawna smiled, reached into the bowl of popcorn

and sat back on Kia's bed. "This is fun. We haven't done it in ages. Remember our Friday-night make-over parties? We were going to open our own beauty shop. You'd do facials and manicures and I'd do hair."

"Yeah, well, guess what? My dreams went down the tube when Diana told me I'd have to do pedicures too. Yuck." Kia plugged her nose. "Think of all the toe jam and stinky feet."

Shawna made a face. "And did you hear about the hairdresser who went home after work and found head lice squirming around under her fingernails?"

"No way!"

Shawna laughed. "No. I just made that up."

Kia grinned and chucked a piece of popcorn at her. But then an awkward silence descended again. Things hadn't been the same between them since the afternoon they'd walked home from school together and Kia had snapped at Shawna. And now Kia was trying to find a way to tell her about the baby, but she just didn't know how. Shawna had been unusually quiet too.

"Is everything okay with you, Ki?"

Kia turned to Shawna, surprised. "Yeah, why?"

"You seem ... I don't know, like, spaced out or something."

"Yeah, well, I guess I am." This was the moment. She sat up, took a deep breath and opened her mouth to break the news, but Shawna interrupted her.

"And Derek's been spreading some ugly rumors about you."

"He has?" This was news. Kia forgot for the moment about telling Shawna anything.

Shawna wouldn't make eye contact with her. "He's saying that you're a slut."

"I don't believe it!" Kia felt the blood rush to her face. "To who?"

"To everyone, it seems like. I heard it from Courtney, who said she heard it from Fahreen. And Lauren said she heard him say so himself. At Mitch's party."

"I'm going to kill him!"

Shawna reached for more popcorn.

"Mitch had a party?"

"Apparently. But don't feel bad," Shawna said. "Lauren said he only invited people who were into weed."

"Lauren's smoking it now too?"

"Yeah. She'll do anything to get Mitch to like her."

"Huh."

"So, how are you going to kill him?" Shawna asked, eyes narrowed. "Why don't you ask him his preference? Slow and painful or ...?"

Kia shook her head. She couldn't see any humor in it. "Why is he saying that stuff? And what does that make him?"

Shawna fluffed up her pillow and pulled the covers up to her chin. "He's a jerk. Everyone knows that. Don't worry about it. No one will believe him."

But Kia knew that wasn't true. Derek had the kind of charm that was powerful, almost hypnotic, and she knew she wasn't the only one who was a sucker for it.

Shawna snooped in the drawer of Kia's night table while she waited for Kia to change into pajamas. She spotted the new journal and picked it up.

"Have you written in this yet?"

Kia nodded numbly.

"Any great words of wisdom?" Shawna didn't open it, but waited expectantly.

Suddenly Kia knew exactly how to break the news to Shawna. "Listen, Shawn, I think if you read what's in there ..." she glanced at the journal, "then you'll understand why I've seemed spaced out."

Shawna tilted her head. "Are you sure? I don't have to."

"Yeah, go ahead, read it," Kia said, walking toward the door. "I'll go make us some hot chocolate. I'll be back in a minute."

When Kia came back into the room carrying two mugs a few minutes later, she found Shawna sitting up, the journal closed in her lap, her face long and pale. She climbed off the bed, crossed the room and hugged Kia, who had to struggle to keep from spilling the hot chocolate down her back.

"Why didn't you tell me sooner?" Shawna asked.

"Because I didn't want you to say I told you so," Kia answered, handing Shawna a steaming mug.

"And did I say that?" Shawna asked, looking hurt.

"No, I'm only kidding," Kia said, realizing too late the sting in her words.

They sat for a moment, Shawna on the bed, Kia in a chair, staring at each other. Finally, Shawna broke the painful silence. "A swarm of bees?"

Kia nodded, then grinned. "Killer bees."

Shawna smiled, setting free a tear. She wiped it away, set her mug on the dresser, then pulled the quilt back for Kia. "Come on, girl. I want to hear everything."

~ fingernails are fully formed
~ baby has reflexes
~ all 20 teeth are formed

Feb. 17

Words.

My parents use words for everything. Talk everything to death. Everything is debated or discussed. They show their feelings through words.

School is about words.

Even Youth Group is about words. I feel blah blah blah. You feel blah blah blah.

Borrring.

Derek was not about words. He was about something else. Energy, desire, heat. I discovered something in me, something instinctual. Something powerful. Something beyond words.

But maybe a few words would have helped. Clarified things. Made me realize we weren't in the relationship for the same thing. Maybe we weren't even in a 'relationship.'

Derek doused my fire, quickly, unexpectedly.

God, how I miss it.

∼

From: Kia <hazelnut@hotmail.com>
To: Justin <justintime@yahoo.com>
Date: Feb. 18
Subject: heavy sigh

hi justin, 2 down, one to go. shawna and angie know.
derek doesn't, and I'm in no hurry to tell him. shawna was
cool, angie was ... i dunno. real quiet. i'm not sure what she
was thinking. all she really said was "who's the dad going
to be?" i told her there wasn't one, and she just looked at
me kinda funny. i really feel like i've let her down, more
than anyone else. i've been like her role model, u know?
and the harassment she's gonna get from her friends will
be brutal. i wonder if mom & dad have told their friends. i
don't have the guts to ask.

what have I done to them?
why?
see ya tomorrow at youth group
k

From: Justin <justintime@yahoo.com>
To: Kia <hazelnut@hotmail.com>
Date: Feb. 18
Subject: Re: spect

hi kia, i don't have any little brothers or sisters, but i know
all about letting people down. been there, done that. it's a
tough one, but in the end you've just got to remember not
to let yourself down. and you're doing great. you're doing
what's right for you, and you're being honest with everyone else. eventually angie will respect that.

can i break the news at youth group?
uncle J

From: Kia <hazelnut@hotmail.com>
To: Justin <justintime@yahoo.com>
Date: Feb. 18
Subject: Re: Re: spect
gladly! C U there.
k & p

Justin struck a match and lit the candle in the chalice
that sat on the floor in the center of their circle. "We
kindle the flame as a symbol of our gathering," he said.

"May the light of understanding illuminate our dark-
ness," the gathered teens in the youth group responded.
"May the warmth of sharing bring us peace."

Justin sat back. "Okay. Check-in time. Who wants
to start?"

"I want to start," Chris said, "by offering some food."
He reached into a paper grocery bag that sat on the floor
beside him and pulled out a tub of once-frozen chocolate
cookie dough and a handful of spoons. "It will be a kind of
... communion, you know? Like they do in other churches."

"Oh yum!" Laurel said.

Chris handed a spoon to each person. "I thought we
could just pass the bucket around while we did check-in.
What do you think?" he asked.

There were enthusiastic nods around the circle.

"You call that food?" Justin asked, smiling.

"Absolutely!" Chris answered, taking the first scoop
and passing the bucket on. "The best kind."

"Food of the gods," Meagan agreed, digging in and
then sucking the gooey chocolate dough off her spoon. She

closed her eyes and tilted her head back. "Ahh. To die for."

Kia settled back and listened to everyone's news as they took turns sharing their stories of the past week. When the bucket reached her, she dug out a rounded spoonful of cookie dough, popped it in her mouth and then passed the bucket to Justin, who was sitting on the floor to her left. His turn to share was next. She was to be last, but she'd have nothing to say. Justin was going to say it for her.

While Chris rattled off the scores of his last four hockey games, Kia glanced sideways at Justin's profile and felt an unexpected fluttering sensation in her stomach. Justin shifted his position just then, stretching out his legs, and his shoulder pressed against hers. She froze. This was not nerves, she realized with alarm, recognizing the feeling.

"So, Chris, are you done?" Justin asked. She felt him shift again, sitting up straighter now. Immediately she missed the warm feel of his shoulder pressed against hers.

"Yeah, that about sums up my week," he answered.

"Okay then, my turn," Justin said. "And have I got news!" He glanced down at Kia and smiled. She felt the fluttering sensation return, but again, it was not nerves.

"I'm an uncle," he declared, grinning and looking around at the group.

"How can you be?" Laurel asked after a moment. "You're an only child."

"Yeah, well, not a real uncle." He looked down at Kia and they made eye contact. She nodded. "Kia is pregnant, and I've made myself 'acting' uncle for the duration of her pregnancy."

There was a stunned silence and Kia felt everyone's eyes on her. Laurel finally found her voice. "Are you really, Kia?"

Kia glanced at her and nodded. Then she looked around at the other eight faces. The expressions were changing from shock to sadness.

"And you're going to have the baby?" Laurel asked. She seemed to be the only one who could speak.

Kia nodded

"Did you consider ..." Meagan couldn't say the word, but they all knew what she meant.

"Yeah, I did. I almost had an abortion, but I changed my mind."

"Are you a pro-lifer or something?" Meagan was the same age as her, Kia realized, and couldn't get her head around the idea of going through with a pregnancy.

Kia shrugged. "I'm not pro-anything. I just couldn't do it."

"Chickened out?" Chris asked softly.

"No, that's not it," Kia answered, her face flushing. "I wasn't scared." She hesitated. "Well, yeah, I was. But I was going to do it anyway when I suddenly realized that it wasn't the right thing for me. I'd been pressured into it, and I knew that was the wrong reason to have one." The room was quiet, so Kia turned back to Meagan. "I guess I am pro-choice, but you know, when people talk about choice, they're usually talking about a woman's right to abortion. I think choice can also mean continuing with an unexpected pregnancy."

"Perhaps there's a big difference between an unexpected pregnancy and an unwanted one," Justin suggested.

"Maybe," Kia said, "though not really in my case. I'd rather not be pregnant, but I'm going to make the best of it. And I'm going to try not to care what anyone else thinks or says." Kia realized she felt better just saying the words out loud. She glanced at Justin, wondering if he remembered suggesting them to her.

He smiled and winked.

"I don't care what any of you think," Laurel blurted out. Kia noticed the defiant set of her jaw. "Abortion is murder, no matter what you call it." She turned to face Kia. "You did the right thing."

Kia felt a tremor run through the small group. Justin must have felt it too. "Let's leave that discussion for another day," he said, sensing the unspoken emotion that was building in the room. "This isn't the time."

Everyone was quiet for a moment. Laurel twisted a strand of hair around and around her finger. Finally Chris spoke up. "Are you going to keep going to school?" he asked.

"Yep."

Chris nodded thoughtfully. The group grew quiet again.

"Please keep in mind our promise to each other," Justin reminded the somber group. "We have a safe circle here, we can talk about anything, but what we talk about here is private. It doesn't go beyond this circle."

No one spoke for a moment, and then the questions came out, one by one.

"Do you have a boyfriend?"

"Not anymore." Kia's eyes dropped, but not before she saw the surprised expressions that crossed everyone's faces, especially Chris's, who went to the same school as her.

"Why weren't you using birth control?"

"We were."

"What kind?"

"A condom. It must have been defective or something."

"Did he have it on right?" Mike asked.

"Yeah. Duh."

"I just thought you might have missed that class."

"What class?"

"The one in Sex Ed," Mike reminded her. "Where we had to practice putting them on bananas." A giggle ran through the group as they recalled the game.

"Yeah, I was there. My team won the relay," Kia quipped.

"Have you told your parents?" Meagan asked. The mood grew serious again.

"Yeah. That was brutal."

There were nods and murmurs around the circle. Justin gently rubbed her back. She wished he'd never stop.

Kia continued. "My dad tried talking me into an abortion too."

"So what are you going to do with the baby?" Meagan asked. She lay stretched out on her tummy, her chin cupped in her hands.

"I don't know yet." Her arms involuntarily crossed over her stomach.

"Are you thinking of keeping it? Really?"

Kia shrugged.

"Was it worth it?" Mike asked.

"Huh?"

He smiled, teasingly. "The sex part."

Everyone groaned and Chris elbowed him in the ribs, but they all turned to Kia to hear the answer.

"No. Not for me. He might think so because he's not pregnant."

"What about if you hadn't got pregnant?" Mike asked.

"Okay, Mike, now you're out of line," Justin said over the noise of the others heckling Mike. "Does anyone have anything else they'd like to ask Kia?"

The room grew quiet again. Then Laurel cleared her throat. "We're here for you, Ki." She looked around at the others and they all nodded. "You know that, right?"

Kia swallowed hard and smiled at her. She felt tears welling up in her eyes.

"And I want to know if I can be an uncle too," Chris asked.

"And I'm the aunt, okay Ki?" asked Meagan.

Justin rested his hand on Kia's shoulder. "How about if we're all unofficial aunts and uncles?" he suggested. "One big, happy family."

Kia could only nod and wipe her eyes. Then, one by one, they crossed the circle and hugged her. There were tears spilling down many of their cheeks by the time they were finished, and Kia knew that it was, truly, a safe circle.

⌒

Kia found Grace waiting near the door of the parlor when she tried to leave after her next piano performance. She smiled politely and attempted to slip past, but Grace maneuvered her wheelchair so she was blocking the doorway.

"Hi, Kia," she said.

"Hi, Grace."

"That was lovely music you played for us today."

"Thanks." Kia smiled and tried to squeeze around the wheelchair.

"Will you stay and have a cup of tea with me, dear?" Grace asked.

Kia glanced at her watch, feeling nauseous at the thought of staying here any longer than she had to, but when she looked into Grace's earnest old face, she found she didn't have the heart to say no.

Kia pushed Grace down to the sunroom. They sat at a table by the window, overlooking an expanse of grass that sloped down to the river in the distance. Kia watched as Grace clamped her mug between both hands and shakily brought it up to her mouth. She took a sip and then slowly, painfully, returned the mug to the table.

"The music was a little more optimistic today, Kia, but not exactly happy."

Kia took a sip of her own tea. "You're one observant lady."

"I have a lot of time for observing. And reflecting. And I tried to think of all the things that could make a girl like you so serious."

"I'm not always serious."

"I know that, from the first few times you played for us. From your selections then, I sensed you were a young lady with a great sense of humor."

Kia studied Grace, intrigued by the old woman's uncanny way of reading her personality through the music she chose to play. She'd never thought about it, but it made sense. She probably did choose music to match her mood.

"Let me guess," Kia teased. "You were a gypsy in a past life. The kind that reads fortunes in tea leaves."

"You're right, Kia." Grace's smile lit up her eyes. "And how did you know that?"

"A woman's intuition." She smiled back, beginning to enjoy herself.

"Ah yes. I know all about intuition."

"Yeah?" Kia asked. "What do you know?"

"I know that you have something weighing heavily on your mind." Grace's sharp eyes caught and held Kia's.

"Really." It was a statement.

"Yes. And I know that you're starting to accept the situation. But you're not exactly happy yet."

"Yeah, Grace, you do have good intuition." Kia narrowed her eyes and tilted her head. "Either that or you've been talking to Justin."

Grace ignored the accusation. "I would venture to guess that the problem might be tall, dark and handsome."

Kia laughed. "Close, but not quite. He's blue-eyed and blond. Has Justin been dropping hints?"

"Nope. Justin hasn't said a thing. Your music says it all."

"You're pretty smart, Grace."

"Oh no. But I think I read people pretty well."

Kia nodded. They both sipped their tea.

"Why don't you tell me about him?" Grace asked, after successfully managing to maneuver her mug back to the table again.

"What do you want to know?"

"Everything. I have nothing but time."

Kia smiled and thought about her answer. "He has ... something. I don't know what the word is, but he made me feel amazing. When we were together I felt ... I don't know. Completely wrapped up in him. I thought maybe that was what love was," she admitted. "But," she added more softly, "now I know he never felt the same about me."

"Love is an imprecise word, isn't it?" Grace said, her voice warbling a little. "One word simply can't describe all the kinds of love in this world, but each kind of love is valid when you're the one experiencing it."

Kia nodded, thinking of Derek, wondering what he had felt for her. "I think the worst part is I'm feeling so stupid. And used. I'd thought he felt the same way."

"It's hard to measure what someone else is feeling."

"But he's the one who started it," Kia argued. "And there seemed to be such a strong attraction between us. I was sure of it. But then when..."

Grace leaned forward, listening carefully.

Kia spoke softly. "But once we'd..."

"Ahh." Grace nodded understanding. "Men like him have been around since my day. Is he charming and good-looking?"

Kia nodded.

"Do girls go all goofy when he's around?"

"Yep."

"Mr. Charismatic?"

"I don't know exactly what that means, but probably."

Grace smiled sadly and rested a hand on Kia's arm. "You know, in some ways I feel sorry for people like that."

"You what?!"

"I do," she said, sitting back in her chair. "For some men, and for some women too, it's the hunt that has all the appeal. They're like spoiled housecats who chase birds and mice because they like the game, but once they capture their prey the thrill is over and they just spit them out and leave them to lick their wounds."

Kia remembered her journal entry. *He was watching me, like a cat watches its prey.*

"So why do you feel sorry for them?" Kia asked.

"Because they never learn to build relationships or develop character. By the time we're adults, most of the rest of us can see through that superficial charm. And then, when they get older and their good looks fade, what have they got? Nothing!"

Kia smiled. "I'm glad to hear that."

"It's just my theory."

"Sounds good to me." Kia took one last sip of her tea and made a face, realizing it was cold. Then she looked around the room. "So where's Justin today?"

"I saw him leave with his friend shortly before you got here. They probably went out for an early supper."

"Oh." His friend. A girlfriend or just some guy? She considered hanging around longer, hoping to find out, but then realized how tired she was. Fatigue was an on-going problem these days.

"I guess I better go, Grace," she said, patting the old woman on the hand and realizing that it no longer repulsed her. "Let's have tea again next week."

Grace's eyes shone. "It's a date," she said.

week 14/40

~ baby produces urine and is urinating into amniotic fluid
~ fingers and toes have separated, nails are growing,
and hair
~ baby breathes the amniotic fluid in and out of its lungs
~ size of a fist

Feb. 24

Was I blind? Why could I not see through Derek before?
Even Grace figured him out, and she's never even met
him!
But even now, I get a little rush when I think of him,
and how it felt to be with him.
What is the matter with me???

~

Kia was surprised to see her mom's car in the driveway
when she arrived home the following day. She found her
sitting alone in the family room.

"Where's Angie?"

"I haven't picked her up yet," her mom answered. "I
wanted a chance to talk to you alone."

"Oh, okay," Kia said, avoiding her mother's eyes as
she dropped her book bag on a chair and pulled open the
fridge door in the kitchen. "What do you want to talk
about?"

"I think you can figure that out."

Kia grabbed a container of yogurt and a spoon and then returned to the family room. She sat across the room from her mom. "I guess you want to talk about my baby."

Her mom nodded but didn't say anything else. She just watched absently as Kia ate.

"Well?" Kia asked finally. "What exactly do you want to talk about?"

Her mother cleared her throat, seeming to drag herself back to the present. "I'm glad you chose not to have that abortion."

Kia looked up, surprised. "Really?"

Her mom nodded, studying her fingers. "I didn't want to say anything around Dad. There's stuff he doesn't know."

Kia sat very still, watching her mom.

"As you know, honey, I grew up in a religious family in the Philippines."

Kia nodded.

"But my dream was always to emigrate to Canada and start a new life."

"And you did."

"I did. But I almost didn't."

"How come?"

"Because I got pregnant."

"Oh." Kia's eyes grew wide. "You don't have to tell me this stuff, Mom."

"Actually, I do. It's been eating away at me for years. And when you said you were pregnant, the horror of it all came rushing back."

Kia put the yogurt container down and sat back,

WABASH CARNEGIE PUBLIC LIBRARY

curling her legs beneath her. She waited patiently for her mom to continue.

"I'd grown up believing, as everyone in my community did, that abortion was a sin."

Kia nodded.

"But I wanted so desperately to move to Canada. It was all I thought about for years, since the oldest sister of one of my friends moved here and used to write letters home about Canada, describing her new life. It sounded like such an adventure. I was counting the days till I could go too."

Kia's mom twisted her wedding band around and around on her finger while she talked. "When I told my boyfriend that I was pregnant, he thought we should get married right away. But he wanted to stay in the Philippines, with his family. He was training to be a police officer, and there was a good job waiting for him when he was done."

Kia nodded, fascinated by her mother's story.

She continued, speaking slowly and deliberately. "It was a horrible time for me. I knew that if I married him and had that baby I would never get to Canada. But not marrying him was not an option because I was pregnant." She paused. "So, I never told my boyfriend what I decided to do. I found a doctor willing to do an abortion—a difficult thing in those days—and went ahead with it. I didn't tell anyone what I had done, I just said I had miscarried. It was awful. I had nightmares and the guilt was devastating."

"But you made it to Canada," Kia said gently. "You met Dad and had us. So aren't you glad you did what you did?"

Kia's mom nodded, but she looked on the verge of

tears. "Everything did turn out the way I planned. And even though your dad and I have found a new spiritual home, one that embraces our different beliefs, the lessons from my childhood are still firmly embedded. Abortion still feels wrong to me on an emotional level, although I can certainly justify it in an intellectual way."

Kia nodded. "Why didn't you tell Dad about this?"

"I don't really know. I guess I hoped that if I buried the guilt deep enough it would go away." She shook her head. "It doesn't. And when it resurfaces it hurts almost as much as it did in the beginning."

Kia got up, crossed the room and sat beside her mom. "So why are you telling me?" she asked quietly.

Her mom sighed deeply. "I find it so strange that you've followed in my footsteps this way. I can't help but think it's more than coincidence."

"I didn't even know about you!" Kia argued.

Her mom nodded. "I know. But at one time I would have thought that your getting pregnant was my punishment."

"Oh, Mom. You don't believe that stuff anymore."

"Not in my head. No." She tapped her temple. "But the stuff you learn in your childhood has a way of staying in your heart a long time. Possibly forever."

"Well, Mom, trust me," Kia said, smiling a little. "I got pregnant all by myself. Well, actually, not all by myself," she blushed, "but you had nothing to do with it."

Mrs. Hazelwood reached out and ran a finger down her daughter's cheek. "Deep down I know that," she said, clasping her hands together and putting them in her lap, "but I needed to share my story with you." There was a long silence, and Kia couldn't remember when she'd ever felt so close to her mom.

"But speaking of Derek ..."

"What about him?" Kia rolled her eyes.

"You told us that this was none of his business."

"It isn't."

"That's where you're wrong, honey. It's as much his baby as it is yours."

"Yeah, right, Mom. You didn't think that when you made your decision ..." Kia stopped, immediately regretting her words.

"That's just my point, Kia." The tone of her mother's voice had changed, losing the warmth of the moment before and beginning to sound authoritative again. "He did deserve to know. That's a big part of the guilt I'm feeling."

"It's different with me." Kia moved away from her mother on the couch. "Derek's had his say. He wanted me to abort it. That tells me he wants nothing to do with it."

"You can't leave him out of this, Kia. It's his responsibility too. Have you told him yet?"

"Not yet," she sighed. "I haven't had the chance."

"Then you better make the chance. And you better do it soon."

Kia realized that the intimate mood they'd just shared was lost. They were back to being mother and daughter again. Sighing, she picked up her yogurt container and spoon and left the room.

~

Kia could hear the sounds of crying from outside when she stopped by Angie's daycare to pick her up. When a preschooler opened the door, the noise got even louder.

"Oh hi, Kia," said Mrs. Jacobs. She came rushing down the hall with one of the crying babies on her hip. "We're having one of those days around here."

"What's the matter?" Kia asked, shutting the door behind her.

"Oh, they're mostly sympathy cries," the woman said calmly. "One or two of them aren't feeling well and their crying sets everyone else off. Here, could you hold Kade?" she asked, passing Kia the baby without waiting for an answer. "I'll help Angie collect her things."

But the baby did not want to be held by Kia. His wails grew even louder as Mrs. Jacobs headed back down the hall. Kia clung onto the squirming bundle, but felt repulsed by the stream escaping from his nose. She tried to position him so none of it would rub onto her, but with his thrashing, it was hard. She found it difficult to believe that this was the same passive little guy she'd played peek-a-boo with when she'd come by yesterday.

She felt a tug on her jacket and looked down. The boy who had opened the door was looking up at her. "Can you help me with this puzzle?" he asked, holding out a handful of wooden pieces.

"I can't right now," Kia said. "Maybe another day." But then she watched in alarm as his eyes too filled with tears. His face crumpled up, and then another wail was added to the commotion.

Mrs. Jacobs returned with Angie and yet another sobbing baby in her arms. "This one just needs a diaper change," she explained, noting Kia's expression. "Not to worry."

Angie tugged on her shoes and picked up her backpack.

"See you tomorrow, Angie," Mrs. Jacobs said as they headed out through the door. She stood on the landing watching them go, a baby on each hip.

"See ya," Angie answered, not even turning to wave. She began to walk quickly, leaving Kia behind.

"How does Mrs. Jacobs manage when everyone cries?" Kia asked, following her sister down the sidewalk.

Angie didn't answer. She just kept walking.

Kia sighed. "Why don't we talk about it?" she suggested, working to keep up. She'd been unable to penetrate Angie's stony silence since she'd broken the news of her pregnancy to her. True to her word, she'd picked Angie up every day after school, but Angie acted like she'd rather Kia hadn't.

Angie shook her head and kept walking. Kia was just about to try another approach when the sound of squealing tires rounding the corner behind them made her stop and turn. She tensed. The racket of the boom box in the approaching gray car was way too familiar. She turned and starting walking faster, urging Angie to keep up.

Derek pulled up beside them, leaned across the seat and pushed open the passenger door.

"Hop in, ladies," he said.

"No thanks." Kia put her arm around Angie's shoulder and kept walking.

The car kept pace with them, the door still swinging open. "I said hop in, Kia," he repeated, a hard edge in his voice.

"And I said no thanks," Kia replied, pushing Angie ahead of her.

"Okay," Derek said, "have it your way. You walk, I

drive. But we talk." Derek had one hand on the steering wheel but was leaning toward the open door. He had to shout to be heard above the music. "I just came to find out how everything went last week."

Kia kept walking, staring straight ahead. She didn't want to have this conversation in front of Angie.

"I asked you a question," he shouted.

Kia stopped. It seemed the chance her mom had referred to was here. She fished around in the bottom of her book bag, looking for her house key. "Go on ahead," she told Angie, handing it to her. "I'll be there in a few minutes."

Angie studied Derek with her serious brown eyes. She turned to Kia and shook her head.

"It's okay, Angie," Kia said. "I'll get rid of him."

Angie didn't move.

"Really, Angie. I'll be right behind you."

Angie hesitated, shrugged and then walked slowly up the sidewalk. Kia watched her for a moment and then reluctantly climbed into Derek's car. She left the door open for a quick escape. "We'll talk right here. Shut it off."

Derek regarded her, considering her request. He took too long. Kia began to climb out of the car.

"Okay already. Get back in." He put the car in park, turned off the engine, but left the music playing. He flung his arm over the back of the seat. Kia climbed back in, pulled her door shut and then leaned over and shut off the stereo.

"Testy, aren't we," he commented.

"What do you want?" she asked.

"I'm just checking up on you. How did it go?"

Kia knew he wasn't concerned about her. He was just making sure she'd gone through with the abortion.

It crossed her mind, fleetingly, that she shouldn't be alone with him when he found out. She turned and studied him. The pale blue eyes were hard and cold, but this was the guy she'd thought she loved not so long ago. Somewhere deep inside of him he must still have feelings for her too. It would be okay.

"New shirt?" she asked, noticing the Hilfiger crest on his chest. She shook her head and smiled to herself. She could almost hear the swarm of bees in the back of her mind ...

"What's the joke?" he asked, watching her carefully.

"Last week went fine," she said, ignoring his question. "For the baby. I'm still pregnant."

She watched his face. It took him a moment to understand what she'd said. Finally, she could see the truth register. "You didn't have it?" he asked, incredulously.

"That's right. I'm still pregnant."

"Why the hell didn't you have it?!"

"I couldn't go through with it," she said. There was no point trying to explain her feelings to him. He'd never understand.

"I knew I should have gone with you," he said, his voice trembling with anger. He turned the key in the ignition. "We have to go make another appointment."

Kia reached for the door handle, but he flung the car into gear and squealed away from the curb before she could get it open.

"Let me out, Derek! I can't leave Angie alone."

Derek pressed harder on the accelerator. There was a red light at the next intersection, so he was forced to slow down and then stop. Kia desperately hoped the light would stay red. She still had her hand on the door handle, but the light turned green almost immediately. Kia yanked up on the handle anyway and pushed the door open with her shoulder. Derek reached over and grabbed for her jacket, but she pulled herself loose and quickly hopped out of the car. She turned and kicked the door shut.

There were no other vehicles coming, so Kia stood at the side of the road and waited to see what Derek would do next. Keeping his eyes firmly locked on hers, he threw the car into reverse and squealed backwards. Before she could react, she found the car bearing down on her. At the last moment Derek yanked on the steering wheel and veered away. In her alarm, Kia jumped backwards and tripped on the curb. The next thing she knew she felt herself hitting the pavement.

"Are you all right?" asked a woman walking along the sidewalk with a small boy.

"I'm okay," Kia answered, struggling to her feet and glancing at Derek's car as it squealed around the corner. She stepped up onto the sidewalk and brushed herself off.

The woman studied Kia, frowning. "Who was that?" she asked.

Kia shook her head. "Just some idiot I know."

"I don't think you should take any more rides with him," the small boy said.

"No, I won't," she answered. "Trust me." She rubbed her right shoulder. It had taken most of the impact of the fall, but she could still rotate her arm so she knew nothing was broken. Her palms were scraped and one knee ached. She took a deep breath. She hoped she hadn't hurt the baby in any way. Wouldn't that be ironic, she thought, if

Derek caused her to have a miscarriage? She shook her head and started walking away. She had to get home to Angie.

"You're sure you're going to be okay?" the woman called after her.

"Yeah, thanks," Kia answered, turning back. Then she realized, with a sinking feeling, that she'd left her book bag in Derek's car. This wasn't over yet.

With a slight hobble, Kia began to retrace the short journey she'd just taken in Derek's car.

From: Kia<hazelnut@hotmail.com>
To: Justin<justintime@yahoo.com>
Date: Feb. 26
Subject: derek knows 2

it didn't go so well — i just finished bailing out of his car, but i'm ok. really. i haven't heard the last from him, but i'm glad he knows.

C U

From: Justin< justintime@yahoo.com >
To: Kia< hazelnut@hotmail.com >
Date: Feb. 26
Subject: Re: derek knows 2

i'm glad you're ok and i'm not justifying whatever it was he did, but u know, despite your feelings about the guy, it is his baby too, and he's impacted by what you're doing.
regardless of what u eventually choose to do with it, he will have a 'child' out there. that's a pretty mind-boggling thought for anyone.

C U tomorrow!
Uncle J

"Haven't you got any homework tonight, Kia?" asked her dad after dinner that night. Without being asked, she'd begun loading the dishwasher and putting away the leftover food. She realized, too late, that her behavior looked suspicious.

"Yeah, but I left my book bag in Derek's car this afternoon," she admitted. "And I don't want to call him to get it back."

"*Derek's* car?" he asked.

She nodded, and began to fill the sink with water.

"You were in his car, but now you don't want to call him? What's going on, Kia?"

Kia glanced at Angie, sitting at the kitchen table with her homework laid out in front of her. Angie turned her attention back to her books and pretended to concentrate.

"I broke the news about the baby to him. The news that I'm still pregnant."

"Yeah? And?"

"He didn't take it too well. He's really …" Kia paused, looking for a polite term. "Angry."

"Well, I guess so. You told him you were going to …" Now her father glanced at Angie. His voice changed, taking on a placating tone. "How about doing your homework in your room tonight, honey?" he suggested.

Angie slammed her books shut but didn't say anything. She made a point of stomping out, although Kia suspected she was secretly relieved to leave the room. Any talk of the baby made her uncomfortable.

When she'd left, Kia's father continued. "You led

him to believe you were having an abortion, right? Of course he'd be angry. He's feeling deceived."

Kia shrugged. "I guess."

"Deceived and overwhelmed, I would think."

Kia began to wash the dishes.

"So what did he say?"

"Not much. He wanted to go make another appointment right away."

Her father picked up a tea towel and began to dry the dishes. "Can't say I blame him. I suppose you're still not willing to reconsider?" he asked, hopefully.

"No, Dad, I'm not."

"Well," he continued, disappointment apparent in his voice, "he deserves an explanation. And you need to get your books. Why don't you invite him over?"

"Are you serious?"

"Yes, I am."

Kia sighed. "If he comes over, you're not going to say anything to him, are you?"

"Like?"

"Like yell at him for what he did."

"For what *he* did?"

"Okay," she said quietly. "For what *we* did."

"I didn't yell at you, did I?"

"No. Maybe you should have."

"I don't see what good that would have done." Her dad looked down at her. She noticed how tired and sad he appeared. "I think it's a little late for lectures, don't you? And accidents happen. I promise to keep my thoughts to myself."

Kia thought about it. At least if Derek came to her

house he couldn't pull any more stupid moves like he had in the car today. "Okay," she agreed, drying her hands. She went down the hall to her mom's small office and dialed his number.

"Derek, it's me," she said when he answered the phone.

"What do *you* want?" he asked. "Oh, let me guess," he continued, without waiting for an answer. "You came to your senses and you made another appointment."

"We need to talk, Derek. And I need my bag from your car."

"There's nothing to talk about, Kia, until you do what you were supposed to."

"That was a stupid move you pulled today."

"Oh, you want to talk about my driving?"

"No, Derek, you know that's not it. Why don't you come over, bring my book bag, and we'll talk ... about the baby."

"Are you nuts? What's there to talk about? If you want your stupid books come and get them yourself. I have nothing more to say to you."

"This is your baby too, Derek. Doesn't that mean anything to you?"

"Yes, it does, Kia," he said quietly. "It means you and I were a big mistake, right from the start. I misjudged you. I would never have thought you'd do something this stupid."

"Derek ..."

"I have nothing more to say. Get an abortion, then we'll talk."

The phone went dead. Kia hung up and slumped in the chair. A moment later she sensed her father standing in the doorway.

"Well?" he asked. "Is he coming over?"

"No. He's too busy right now." Kia didn't know why she was covering up for him.

"Do you want me to take you over there then, to get your books?"

"Yeah, thanks."

When they arrived at his house she found her bag outside the front door. She picked it up, grateful not to have to see him, and climbed back into her father's car. They rode home in silence. When they pulled into the driveway, her father patted her knee and said, "He'll come around."

"Maybe."

"He will. You'll see. Finding out you're going to have a baby is quite a shock."

Kia nodded. "I know."

⁓

Feb. 26

I hate him, hate him, hate him.

I hate that my baby is half him.

Will I hate my baby if she looks like him?

How could I ever have found that shallow jerk so ... oh god, so perfect?

Was it just a physical attraction? Am I that shallow too?

Oh god. I hate me too.

the second trimester

Justin took Kia's hand as they approached the community center where the first prenatal class was being held. She looked up at him, surprised.

"I'm your partner," he said. "Okay?"

She nodded, noticing how warm his hand was against her cold one.

"And partner can mean just about anything these days," he said. "So it's not really a lie."

Kia nodded again. Partner. She liked the sound of it.

Dr. Miyata had been right about the prenatal class—there was an interesting mix of expecting couples there. All skin colors were represented, and there was a wide range of ages. Some of the women looked old enough to be grandmothers, Kia thought, but no one looked as young as she did.

They were greeted with warm smiles and Kia began to relax. This might not be so bad after all. The couples tended to be holding hands or touching in some way, so Justin put his arm around her and she leaned into him. It felt like the perfect fit.

"Good evening, moms and partners," said Shannon, the prenatal instructor.

"And uncles," Kia whispered. Justin squeezed her shoulder.

"Welcome to our first class," Shannon continued. "We have a lot to talk about tonight. Before we get started, I want each of you to introduce yourselves and tell us how you feel about having a baby."

Kia's stomach knotted up. This was exactly the kind of warm and fuzzy stuff she didn't want to get into. She listened to one couple after another describe, in a gush of emotion, what having a baby meant to them. When it was their turn, Kia introduced herself and then Justin, as her partner. She turned to the next couple, hoping to bypass the "feeling" part, but it didn't work.

"And what are your feelings about the baby?" Shannon asked.

"We've nicknamed it Peanut," Justin said, jumping right in as if he really was the proud father. "And he, I mean she," he winked at Kia, "has a wonderful mother." There was a smattering of applause. Kia felt her face burn, but her heart was racing. "I don't know about Kia," he said, "but I'm in awe of this whole pregnancy and birth thing. It's so miraculous." There was a murmur of agreement all around the room. He looked down at Kia and she nodded at him. She wasn't sure if her pregnancy was miraculous or just a disaster, but she was glad Justin had come to her rescue once again.

⁓

Later, over hot chocolate, Kia thanked him once more for coming along.

"Hey. It was fun," he assured her. "For a few minutes there I forgot that I really wasn't the father." He smiled, but it was a sad smile.

"And I was wishing you really were him too," she said, then quickly corrected herself. "I don't mean him, Derek, I mean him, the real father."

"I knew what you meant."

The warmth she saw in his eyes felt like a hug.

They sat quietly for a few minutes, each lost in thought.

"Having a baby really brings couples closer, doesn't it? There was so much love in that room," Justin commented.

Justin's usual cheeriness was gone and a melancholy thoughtfulness had taken its place. Kia wished she could read his thoughts. What was it about the prenatal class that had made him sad? She stared into her own mug. Did he realize she'd meant what she'd said? That she really did wish he was the father?

She looked up and found him staring at her. She felt herself blush but didn't know why. "I'm afraid I'm going to be awfully attached to this baby by the time it's born," he confessed.

She nodded. "Me too."

"But it's your baby. Not mine."

"That doesn't matter." She studied him, puzzled. He didn't meet her gaze. "Have you changed your mind?" she asked, trying to swallow her alarm. "I wouldn't blame you. You don't have to go through with this prenatal stuff, you know. I'll understand. Honest."

He reached across the table to touch her arm. "No, no," he answered softly. "Nothing like that. I think I'm just experiencing some paternal pangs or something." He smiled, and Kia noticed the light was back in his eyes.

"You'll probably have dozens of your own babies," Kia teased, relief flooding through her. She didn't know what was bothering him, but she knew she wanted him with her for the next six months. And after that …

"How old are you, Justin?" she asked.

"Don't you know it's not polite to ask a person's age?" he teased.

"How old are you?" she repeated.

"Twenty-three, if you really must know."

So, there was six years between them then, which might seem like a lot now, she thought, but it wouldn't be once she was an adult. And if she kept the baby she'd be a parent. How much more adult could you get?

～

"Baseball tryouts are next Saturday," Shawna said.

"What time?" Kia asked. They were walking down the crowded school hallway toward their next class.

"Noon, I think. I wonder if we'll keep the same positions this year."

"I hope so," Kia said. "Last year was so … damn!" She came to a sudden stop and then had to fight her way over to the wall to avoid being trampled by the crowd of students coming up behind her.

Shawna followed. "What?"

"I can't play this year," said Kia.

"Why not?"

Kia watched as realization dawned on her friend's face.

"Oh yeah."

"I forgot all about baseball."

"What are you going to tell the others?"

"The truth, I guess. I know I'm not showing yet, but it's bound to happen soon."

"I guess that means Camp Chewelah is out too."

Kia nodded. "The baby's due at the end of August. I don't think they'll want a junior counselor who's pregnant." She sighed. "I forgot all about that too."

"It was going to be a blast."

"I know. Maybe next summer." Maybe. If she didn't have a one-year-old child. With a heavy heart, Kia followed Shawna into Math class.

March 1
This detour is full of pitfalls.
What's so great about that?
I'm not even a real mom yet, but I've already had to give up so much.
What's the big deal about being a parent anyway?

Kia crossed her legs and gritted her teeth. "I can't hold on much longer. I'm going to explode!"

Justin approached the woman who sat behind the desk at the ultrasound clinic. "Can you tell us how much longer? Kia's not going to make it."

The woman reached under the desk and pulled out a plastic container that resembled a measuring cup. "Perhaps she could void about four ounces. To here," she said, indicating a line on the cup.

"You've got to be kidding!" Kia wailed. "Once I start peeing there'll be no stopping."

Justin stared helplessly at Kia.

"That's it," she said, getting to her feet. "Point the way to the washroom. I've got to go, now."

The door to the ultrasound room swung open and a technician whose name tag identified her as Yvonne stepped into the waiting room. "Are you Kia?" she asked.

"I am, but I'm on my way to the washroom," Kia said. "I can't wait another second."

"Come on in and lie down," Yvonne said. "It will take the pressure off your bladder. You need to have a full bladder to help us see the baby, but the exam will only take a few minutes and then you can go to the bathroom. You've come this far, it would be a shame not to do the ultrasound now."

Kia took a deep breath, clutched the back of her gown together and entered the dark room.

"I'll call you in a moment," Yvonne said to Justin. "Once I've taken the measurements you'll be able to get a sneak preview of your baby."

Justin nodded and returned to his seat.

Kia climbed up on the cot and lay down. Immediately she felt some relief on her throbbing bladder. Yvonne pulled the medical gown up to Kia's navel after covering her from the hips down with a sheet. Kia flinched when the woman squirted a cool gel on her stomach.

"I'm sorry, I know it's cold, but it helps the paddle move." Yvonne placed an instrument on Kia's skin and swirled it through the gel. Then she began to peer into a screen as she slowly moved the paddle around Kia's lower abdomen. Now and again she stopped and pushed some buttons on her computer.

"This is a real active little guy," Yvonne said, rotating

the paddle. "He won't stay still long enough for me to measure him."

"Him?"

"Him or her. I'm not going to tell," she said with a smile. "But *it* is kicking up a storm. A real swimmer." She pushed a little harder on the paddle and studied the screen. Suddenly she hit a couple more keys. "There, got it."

"Is everything okay?"

"Everything looks fine. I'll send the report to your doctor and she can go over it with you. Should I go and get the young man?"

"Sure. Thanks."

Yvonne swiveled the computer screen so it was facing Kia and then went to the door to call Justin. After he had taken a seat, he picked up Kia's hand, and they studied the image on the screen together.

"This is its head," Yvonne said, pointing at a dark area near the top of the screen. She pushed harder on the paddle as she studied the image. "And this is one arm, the other arm, and down here are the legs."

"I can't see anything," Kia said, disappointed.

"Me neither," said Justin.

"Try looking at this area," Yvonne suggested. "I've got it magnified so that what you see is bigger than what it is. Oh, look! It's just put a hand to its mouth. I bet it's sucking its thumb!"

"Oh, I see it!" Justin exclaimed. He pointed at something on the screen. "Look, Kia, the back is curved quite a bit and its head is facing down."

"Huh? All I see are black clouds moving in and out on the screen."

Yvonne used an arrow to point to a dark area. "This is the back of its head," she said, "and the neck is here." She drew a line on the screen. "This is the spine and this dark mass is the heart beating …"

"Yes! I see it!" Kia squinted at the screen. "She does look like she's sucking her thumb. Totally weird. We're actually seeing my baby. This is so cool!"

Justin took her hand again. After watching the baby's movements for a minute, Kia glanced at Justin and noticed that the sad smile from the other night was back on his face. She squeezed his hand. He glanced at her and suddenly the little-boy grin was back where it belonged.

"Look! She's waving at us," Justin said. "Wave back, Kia," he said, waving at the screen himself. "Wave at your baby."

She laughed, but joined him in waving at the dark mass on the screen.

Yvonne smiled as she removed the paddle from Kia's abdomen and wiped off the gel.

"All right, now I really do have to pee," Kia said. "You better get out of my way, Justin, or there's no saying what may happen."

He stood and backed up against the wall, putting up his hands in self-defense. Yvonne turned on the lights and Kia pulled her gown back down, tugged the sheet out from under it and leapt off the cot.

"It's down the hall on your left," Yvonne called at the retreating figure. She handed Justin a print of the image they'd just seen on the screen. "Your son," she said. "Or daughter," she added, laughing at his astonished face.

week 15/40

~ she sucks her thumb
~ she's the size of a softball
~ baby empties bladder every 40-45 minutes

March 5

A picture <u>is</u> worth a thousand words.

I've seen her. She's real. This detour is worth every extra mile, pitfalls and all!

I don't care about baseball or summer camp. I'm busy growing a baby. She's all there. I am creating her. It is so amazing.

And Justin is there with me.

From: Kia <hazelnut@hotmail.com>
To: Justin <justintime@yahoo.com>
Date: March 7
Subject: help!

it happened. i couldn't zip the zipper on my jeans today. this is going to be so weird. i've never been fat. so where is a good used clothing store? mom says she's not paying for expensive clothes i'll only wear for 6 months.

K (in sweat pants)

From: Justin <justintime@yahoo.com>
To: Kia <hazelnut@hotmail.com>
Date: March 7
Subject: help is here!
let's go shopping! i'll pick you up on sat. at 11:00. ok?

justinpajamabottoms.

From: Kia <hazelnut@hotmail.com>
To: Justin <justintime@yahoo.com>
Date: March 7
Subject: Re: help is here!
great!!! thanks!!!!

k.

"When is the baby due?" asked Miss Jaswal, the school counselor.

"The end of August." Kia sat in the counselor's office, facing her across a wide desk.

"And you plan to continue attending Creekside for the rest of this year?"

Kia nodded and tugged down on her baggy sweatshirt after observing how neatly Miss Jaswal's pale-blue silk blouse tucked into the waistband of her snug Calvin Klein jeans.

"Senator Ridge High has a special program for teen mothers, you know." Miss Jaswal crossed one long leg over the other and sat back in her chair. "Have you heard of it? You might feel more comfortable switching to that program."

"No. My friends are here. I'm staying."

Miss Jaswal leaned forward. "I understand how you feel now, Kia, but you might find your friends become … how shall I put it?" She crinkled up her eyes. "Less friendly, once your pregnancy becomes more noticeable." She glanced at Kia's stomach. Her teeth were clenched but her lips were splayed in a chimpanzee-like smile. Kia noticed a lipstick smear on her front tooth. "I've seen it happen before," Miss Jaswal continued. "Many times."

"Less friendly?" Kia shook her head. "That won't happen with my friends."

"No? I hope you're right." Miss Jaswal sighed and leaned back in her chair again. "You'd have a lot more in common with those girls—the ones at Senator Ridge …"

"The only thing I'd have in common with them is pregnancy. There's more to me than that."

"Okay," she said. "It's your choice. I'll let your teachers know about your … condition. I guess the only class you won't be able to continue in is PE, depending on the unit. You and Mrs. Kennedy can decide how you will earn your mark. Maybe a report on post-natal fitness or something," she added, glancing again at Kia's stomach. She pushed back her chair and stood up. "Good luck, Kia."

"Thanks," she said. For nothing. Before she closed the door behind her she poked her head back in to the office.

"Yes?" Miss Jaswal asked.

Kia tapped a front tooth with her finger. "Lipstick," she said, crinkling her eyes and splaying her lips in her own chimpanzee imitation.

"Mr. Fairborn won't look me in the eye, and Mrs. Kislanko won't stop staring at me. Ms. Rice tried hard to act like she didn't know anything, and Howie-baby kept giving me a sad look, like I had cancer or something."

"Howie-baby?"

"Yeah. Mr. Howard. You know—Howie-baby. Everyone calls him that. It's because of his baby face, I think."

"I haven't had him," Shawna said, putting the lid on the nail polish and holding her hands up for inspection. "What do you think?" she asked.

"They look great," Kia said, walking away from the table in Shawna's kitchen and opening the window. "But the smell is making me sick. Are you finished?"

"I love the smell of nail polish."

"I used to, but I'm super sensitive to smells right now. It's weird."

"The baby thing?"

"Yeah. And look, Shawna," Kia said, holding up her sweatshirt and pulling down the top of her sweatpants to expose the slight bulge of her stomach. It's growing."

"Huh."

"Huh? Don't you think it's cool?"

Shawna frowned.

"There's a baby growing in me, Shawna! It sucks its thumb. It's kicking." Kia unzipped her book bag and pulled out the picture from the ultrasound. "Look. Here she is." She pointed to the dark shape in the center. "This is her head, her arm, her bum … can you see her?"

Shawna squinted at the fuzzy image. "I guess so. Sort of."

"So now do you think it's cool?"

"Cool? I would never have thought of it that way. But, yeah, sure, I guess ..." Shawna looked away.

Kia sighed. At least Justin had thought it was. "How did ball tryouts go?"

Shawna sat up. "Excellent!" The light was back in her eyes. "We all made it. Except you, of course. Brittney got your spot. But you'll get it back next year."

"Brittney? No way!"

"Yeah, she's an awesome hitter. She must have been working out, because she looked fast running the bases."

"Are we talking about the same Brittney? Brittney Stokes?"

Shawna nodded, pausing before she went on. "Everyone wanted to know where you were."

"Did you tell them?"

Shawna nodded. "You said you were going to tell them the truth."

"I said *I* was going to tell the truth. Not you." There was a hard edge to Kia's voice.

"That's not the way I remember it," Shawna said. "And you weren't there. You wanted me to lie?"

Kia crossed her arms. "How did they react?"

Shawna smiled. "I wish you had seen their faces."

"Yeah?"

"Uh-huh. Total shock. And then someone said, 'Kia? Kia Hazelwood?' Then they all wanted to know who— who the father was."

"Did you tell them that too?"

"No. But someone guessed Derek. Everyone knew you were going out with him for awhile."

"Great."

"The general feeling was shock that you'd actually done it."

"Done it? You mean, like, had sex?"

"Yeah."

"Do I look like the virgin queen or something?"

"No, but you know how it is. Everyone seems to know who has and who hasn't."

"I thought Derek had straightened everyone out with his rumors about me."

Shawna shrugged. "Maybe nobody believed him. The jilted boyfriend syndrome. It would make sense."

Kia nodded. She could make two lists too, one of those who'd had sex and one of those who hadn't. She'd have to remember to move her own name over to the "had" side. Shawna was still a "had not" and seemed to be in no hurry to change her status. Kia hadn't been either, before Derek.

The room grew silent.

"So what did you do today?" Shawna asked finally.

"I went shopping for fat clothes with Justin." Growing a baby had lost its charm in the last ten minutes.

"With Justin? The Youth Group guy?"

"Uh-huh." Kia realized how out of touch she and Shawna had become. "He's been a really good friend for the last few weeks." Kia didn't miss the look that crossed Shawna's face. "You know what I mean. Not the kind of friend that you are, obviously." She touched Shawna's arm. "But he gets his mom's car at nights and on weekends. He's been coming to prenatal classes with me and stuff like that."

"He has?"

Kia nodded. "I didn't want to spend money on new clothes, and he always shops at second-hand stores so he knew where to go."

"What did you find?"

"I found maternity clothes all right, but they are so gross! The pants have this ugly elastic panel thingie at the front or dumb little zippers at the side that you can let out as you grow bigger. All the shirts look like tents and have stupid slogans like 'Baby Under Construction' written on them. I bought a couple pairs of the zipper pants and some guy shirts to go over them. My own sweatpants will work for awhile longer. I guess I'll have to go shopping again when the weather gets warm."

"With Justin?"

"With whoever." Kia studied Shawna's face. "Why?"

"Just wondering," she said, smirking.

Kia threw a cotton ball from the manicure set at her friend. "What are you getting at, Shawna?"

Shawna threw it back. "Doesn't it strike you as just a bit odd that a twenty-something-year-old would want to go shopping with you? He could have told you where the stores were. And prenatal classes? I'd say that's pushing his role as Youth Group leader."

"Twenty-three, actually. And like I said, what are you getting at?"

"I bet he's got the hots for you."

"You think?" Kia picked up a nail file and pretended to study her nails.

"And just maybe," Shawna said, studying Kia's reaction, "you've got the hots for him too."

Kia met Shawna's gaze. "He's the nicest guy I've ever met. That's for sure."

Shawna smiled. "And? Is that a confession?"

Kia felt her skin get hot. "Sort of." She smiled.

"Aha! I knew it!" Shawna grinned.

"There's a few problems."

"And what are those?"

"One, his age. My parents would freak. Two, he is the Youth Group advisor. He's forbidden to have any kind of relationship with anyone in the group, other than platonic."

"Then you just have to quit the group."

Kia laughed. "Yeah. I guess that would work."

"What other problems are there?"

"Well, none I guess. Except for the fact I'm having a baby and I'm going to get fat and look like a cow."

"That won't last forever."

"No, you're right. And you know, I think there's something about this baby that fascinates Justin."

"Really?"

"Yeah, it's weird. He admitted he was already getting attached to it."

"You're right. That is weird."

"Not that weird," Kia said, suddenly defensive. "I'm pretty attached to it too. Just because you aren't ..."

"What's that supposed to mean?"

"Nothing."

Shawna got up and closed the window. "What's he like, anyway? I've never met him."

"He's ... sweet. The complete opposite of Derek. And he's gentle and kind and spiritual and funny."

"A spiritual *guy*? C'mon, Kia!"

"He is, and he's everyone's friend and I bet he's never had an unkind thought. Ever. He sees beauty all around him."

Shawna clutched her throat, gagging. "He sounds weird to me."

"He is," Kia laughed. "But once you get used to him you appreciate his weirdness."

"What does he look like?"

Kia laughed again. "He looks just about as weird as he is. But he's so … centered."

"Centered? Get real!"

"He is. You have to meet him. He radiates a kind of peacefulness."

"Like the great J.C. himself?"

"Yeah. Just like that."

Shawna stared at her friend. "Kia, you've lost it. Getting pregnant has affected your brain."

Kia sighed. "Maybe you're right. But being pregnant has helped me see what's important about a guy and …"

"Maybe you're just growing up."

"Maybe. And you would know, wouldn't you?" Kia put her nose in the air and pressed her lips together. "Miss Maturity herself."

"Or maybe," Shawna said softly, ignoring the comment, "just maybe, you're feeling insecure about being pregnant and he's treating you so nice and he is so different from Derek …"

Kia shook her head.

"And he's older and wiser and …"

"No, Shawna. That's not it."

"And spiritual and sweet …"

"Shut up, Shawn!"

Shawna shut up, but it was too late, Kia realized. The seed of doubt had been planted.

~ fat is forming on baby
~ fingernails are well formed
~ baby is growing hair
~ size of a hand spread wide open

Mar. 12
Shawna is wrong.
He is the perfect partner.
Our feelings are mutual and right.
It can work.
It will work.

Kia stared at her reflection in the bathroom mirror at Jared's house, where the music from the party could be felt more than heard as the walls vibrated. It wasn't just her stomach that was growing, she noticed. Her face seemed rounder, and she'd struggled today to get a ring off her finger. She looked down at her maternity jeans and the sweatshirt that hung over them. She didn't look pregnant yet. Just fat.

The hallway was dark when she opened the door, and she only spotted the figure coming at her as she was shoved back into the bathroom.

"Hey!"

"Kia. How are you?"

"Derek?" She stopped struggling and looked up. "I didn't know you were here."

"Just long enough to see you coming to the bathroom," he said. "Alone." He shut the door and leaned against it. "We need to talk."

Kia felt the hairs on the back of her neck stand up. "I thought you said we didn't have anything to talk about."

"We didn't. But now we do." He reached behind him and locked the door. Then he pointed at her slightly swollen stomach. "So, you never did fix your little problem."

"No, I didn't."

He stood very still, looking down at her. She didn't dare move, and she didn't look away. Then, just when she didn't think she could stand the suspense any longer, he reached out and ever so gently ran his finger along her bottom lip—a gesture he knew used to arouse her. She hadn't seen it coming. Their eyes remained locked as she pushed his arm away. She hoped he hadn't spotted the shock she'd felt when that familiar sensation swept through her. Then she shook her head and looked away. What was the matter with her? How could she feel that with him again, that tingle of excitement?

He moved closer, forcing her to back up. With only a few inches between them she could smell the beer on his breath. She noticed his bloodshot eyes. "That's a shame," he said, "because rumor has it that I'm the father." There was a tremble in his voice that made Kia nervous.

"I never told anyone that." No one except her parents. And Justin. And Shawna.

"No, you didn't have to."

"I heard you'd spread rumors about me anyway. You said that I was sleeping around. Who knows what people think? Who cares?"

"I care. I was ready to do the responsible thing. I took you to the doctor and the counseling session. I would have taken you for the abortion too, if I'd known you were going to chicken out."

"I didn't chicken out." But a twinge of guilt made her look away. She hadn't included him in her decision, and it was his baby too.

He was looking straight down at her, swaying slightly, a sneer plastered on his face. "I'd forgotten how pretty you are, Kia." He leaned forward, forcing her back against the wall. Then, without warning, he pressed his lips against hers, assaulting her with the taste of beer and marijuana. She squirmed to free herself, but he pushed himself even harder against her, pinning her against the wall, his lips crushing hers. She fought desperately to escape, but with his size and weight, she couldn't move. He began to grind his hips into hers.

Rage welled up inside Kia. She tore her mouth away from his and screamed, but the vibration in the wall against her back reminded her how loud the music was. No one would hear anything.

Derek's hands began groping at anything they could reach. He leaned back a little, attempting to tug her sweatshirt up. It gave Kia just the space she needed. She jerked a knee up, hard. Her aim was perfect, nailing Derek in the groin. He stepped back, doubled over, groaning. She scrambled past him and stood at the door, looking down on him.

"Now what is it you wanted to talk about?" she asked.

"Bitch!" he gasped, still doubled over.

"It's too late for an abortion, Derek," she said, watching him closely. "I'm having a baby."

He slumped against the far wall and slid to the floor. Then he covered his face with both hands. "I won't have anything to do with it," he said eventually.

"You don't have to." Kia watched as he drew in great, shuddering breaths.

"What are you going to do with … it?"

Kia noticed he couldn't bring himself to say the word baby. Watching him, she realized the danger was gone. He looked pathetic, crouched there beside the toilet. She leaned against the bathroom door and slid down into a squatting position too. "I don't know yet."

"If you keep it, I won't contribute or anything."

"I'm not asking you to."

He was quiet for a long time. Then Kia watched while he rubbed his face and dropped his hands, but he didn't look at her. "My dad would kill me for getting a girl pregnant." His voice was thick with emotion.

Kia didn't answer. She just sat very still. Finally he looked up at her. She was shocked to see the fear in his eyes. "I'm serious," he said. "He would kill me."

Kia tried to picture Derek's father. She'd only met him once, but he did have an intimidating presence.

"Then he doesn't have to know."

"People talk."

"I'll deny it."

He shook his head. "I don't know …"

"You don't have a choice, Derek."

"You promise not to finger me?" he asked nervously.

Kia was shocked at his expression. Gone was the swaggering big shot that she knew. Now he looked more like a frightened little boy cowering in the corner.

"Your father doesn't have to find out, Derek."

Derek covered his face with his hands again. Kia heard him sniffle and decided that he was more drunk or stoned than she'd thought.

"I'm sorry," she whispered. She opened the door and was about to slip out when he spoke again.

"I'm sorry too, Kia," he said. "But I can't handle it."

"I know." She shut the door and leaned against it. Then, taking a deep breath, she returned to the party and searched for Shawna among the dancing throng. She glanced at the couples leaning against the wall or sitting on the floor around the perimeter of the room. Heads were bent together in conversation—trying to be heard over the music—but Shawna wasn't among them either.

"Have you seen Shawna?" she asked, breaking into one intimate conversation after another. Heads shook, shoulders shrugged. No one paid much attention.

"I saw her with Eric awhile ago." Rochelle looked annoyed at being interrupted. "Maybe they went outside."

"Tell her I left," Kia said. Rochelle nodded vaguely, glanced down at Kia's stomach, then went back to her conversation.

◡

They sat in the Hazelwood living room, Reverend Petrenko, Kia's parents, Kia and Sadie the social worker the Reverend had invited to join them.

"So when is the baby due, Kia?" Sadie asked after accepting a cup of tea from Kia's mom.

"The end of August." Although she didn't want to talk to her, Kia liked the friendly look of this woman, with her gray ponytail and softly lined face. She'd told the Reverend she wasn't ready, but her parents were pressuring him.

"Just talk to her, Kia," he'd said. "You're not committing to anything, but we need to get the ball rolling."

"And you're considering adoption?" Sadie asked.

Kia glanced at her father. He stared back at her. She nodded, but didn't meet Sadie's eyes.

Sadie regarded her thoughtfully, then reached into her canvas satchel. "I have a binder here I can leave with you to look over. It contains information on couples who want to adopt a baby. You'll find out about their work, their hobbies and their religious beliefs, if they have any." She flipped through the pages. "They tell a bit about themselves, their values, and there's also pictures of them. Make a shortlist of the ones who you think would make the best parents and then I can set up interviews with them. Meeting them in person will give you a much better idea of what they're like."

Kia nodded, but she didn't reach for the binder.

"It must be hard for the couples who get interviewed and are not chosen," Kia's mom commented. "They would get their hopes up, I guess. But not all of them ..."

Sadie nodded. "It is hard for them, but I guess it's like any other game. You know before you start that someone is going to win and everyone else is going to lose.

And to get interviewed means you're one step closer to possibly realizing your dream of having a child. Adopting couples like to meet the birth parents too. It takes some of the mystery out of the process."

"What if the birth mom changes her mind at the last minute?" Kia asked. She felt, rather than saw, her father tense.

"The birth mom does have a few weeks to change her mind." Sadie sighed. "It's never easy, Kia, but it does help when you've chosen the adoptive parents yourself. At least you know where your child is going. Not knowing is very painful for many mothers."

"Birth mothers had to rely on blind faith in the old days," the Reverend added. "And we all know how hard that can be," he said, smiling.

"The father will have to sign the adoption papers too, Kia," Sadie said. "Is that going to be a problem?"

She shook her head. "I don't think so."

"Good. I know we've still got a few months, but it will go quickly. It takes time to set up interviews, and often you'll want to meet with couples more than once, so the sooner you get a shortlist to me, the better. Okay?"

Kia noticed that her hands were resting on her stomach again. She quickly folded her arms across her chest. "Okay."

Sadie stood up. "I'm here to help, Kia. And any time you want to chat, about anything, give me a call. My business card is in the front of that binder."

"Thanks."

"That still goes for me too, Kia," the Reverend said, rising and placing a hand on her shoulder.

"I know."

Kia stood at the door with her parents and watched the guests leave. Her father turned to her as he shut the door. "You can do this, Kia."

She swung around to face him. "Could you have given me up for adoption?"

"That's different, Ki," her mom answered, following her up the stairs and into the living room. "You were planned. We wanted you."

"Who's to say I don't want this baby?" She plunked herself on the couch and picked up the binder lying on the coffee table.

"Babies need two parents, Kia, and not just for conception," her dad said quietly, sitting across the room from her. "They are a lot of work." He studied her sullen expression. "Your baby is our grandchild, you know," he added pointedly, "so don't think this doesn't affect your mom and me."

Kia looked up, surprised.

"But we really aren't prepared to raise another child right now," her mom said, sitting down beside Kia.

"I know that."

"So we think that this grandchild will be better off in a home with a couple who have planned to have a child in their lives."

"Lots of kids are raised by single parents," Kia argued.

"That's true," said her mom. "And many single parents do an admirable job of raising well-adjusted kids. But it isn't easy. And there's no time left over for the parent to have a life of their own. We want more than that for you."

Kia began flipping through the pages.

"You'll be seventeen when this child is born." Her

dad picked up the argument. "You'll still want to go to college. You'll want to have a social life. It's so much harder to do those things when you're a single parent."

"I know."

"And financially it's a real struggle. Social assistance helps, but it won't maintain the lifestyle you're used to ..."

"I know that too," she said impatiently. She knew it, but she didn't want to think about it.

She pretended to become absorbed in one of the adopting parents' bio sheets, hoping her parents would leave her alone. They did. She heard her dad pick up a book, and her mother went down the hall to her office.

So, she thought to herself, the main reason her parents didn't think she should keep the baby was because she was going to be a single parent. If she had a partner, someone to raise the baby with ...

Her heart skipped a beat. She knew just the person to do the job, someone as attached to the baby as she was. Would he be willing?

～

They flipped through the binder pages together after prenatal class, in their usual booth at the coffee shop.

"This guy looks like a Hell's Angel," Kia commented. "Who'd pick him for a father?"

"A motorcycle momma," Justin said.

Kia turned the page. "Very funny."

"Look at this one." Justin put his finger on a page. "She doesn't look any older than you."

"Well, she is," Kia said, reading the statistics. "Quite a bit, actually."

"Must be an old picture."

"Must be." Kia snapped the binder shut. "Do you think I'm too young to be a good parent?"

Justin paused, choosing his words carefully. He turned so he was facing her. "I think you'll be a great parent at any age, Kia. That's not really the problem."

"And what do you think the problem is?"

Justin sighed. "Why don't you tell me what you think the problem is?"

"My parents," she said. "And they think the problem is that I'd be a single parent."

"I agree. That is a problem."

Kia folded her arms across her chest. "Why?"

"Because there's so much you need to do before you start raising kids."

"Like what?"

"Like finish growing up. Like having a career. Like having fun. And," he smiled, "like falling in love."

She took a deep breath. "I think I *am* falling in love." She looked him right in the eye.

He continued to smile. "Well, that's good news." He tilted his head. "Who's the lucky guy?"

She kept looking directly at him.

The silence between them filled with understanding.

"You mean the baby, don't you, Ki?" His eyes narrowed, and he spoke firmly, almost roughly. "You're falling in love with the baby."

His words were like a kick to the stomach. Kia nodded and looked away. "Yeah, that's what I mean," she said, swallowing hard.

"Because," he whispered, "if you mean anything else,

don't go there, Kia." He reached over and took her hand between his. "Please."

She nodded, but she could no longer look him in the eye. She pulled her hand away and finished her hot chocolate. Then she glanced at her watch. "I have to go."

"Okay," Justin said. But he didn't move to let her out of the booth.

Finally, she looked him in the eye again.

"I cherish our friendship, Kia. It means a lot to me."

She nodded but looked down again, her hair falling over her face.

"There's stuff you don't know, Kia, but please, don't shut me out."

"It's just that ..."

"Shh. Don't do this." He reached over and tucked her hair behind her ear so he could see her face. Then he put his hand under her chin, lifting it so she had to face him. "I've had ..." He paused, searching for the right word. "Fantasies too. I want to be a father. But it's not going to happen."

"Why not? Why couldn't we raise the baby together?" she asked, hating the desperation in her voice. "You said partner means all different kinds of things. Couldn't we keep on being partners, just like in prenatal class?"

Justin just shook his head.

"Why not?"

"For a million reasons." He dropped his hand. "But we're in this together, and we're going to find the best possible parents for her."

"I thought you were on my side."

"There are no sides, Kia. Just choices."

week 18/40

~ girl baby's ovaries now contain primitive egg cells
~ permanent teeth buds are forming behind the already
formed milk teeth buds
~ pads of the fingers and toes are formed and the
fingerprints are developing
~ size of a honeydew melon

Mar. 24
There are so sides. Me against everyone else.
Why did I say anything? Now that I've said it I can
never go back. It changes everything.

~

Dear Peanut,
    I haven't felt you move yet, but I know you're there
and I luv you. It's so easy for everyone else to tell me I
have to give you up — you are not a part of them. But you
are as much a part of me as my own heart is. There is no
one to talk to anymore. I thought Justin understood. I
thought we had the same feelings for each other.
    I thought wrong. I'm so stupid.

~

"Why'd you leave the party early?" Shawna asked. They were

sitting across from one another at a table in the cafeteria.

"Derek showed up."

"Yeah. So? You go to the same school. You're gonna run into each other."

Kia bit into her apple. She considered telling Shawna what had happened between her and Derek, but decided against it. "I wasn't having much fun."

"Oh."

"I'm feeling kinda fat and frumpy."

Shawna nodded.

Rochelle sat down beside Kia. "Well?" she asked Shawna.

Shawna smiled. "You guess."

"Did he ask you?"

"Maybe," Shawna teased.

Kia frowned. Had she missed something here?

"Tell me!" Rochelle demanded

"Why should I?"

"Shawna!"

Before Kia could ask what it was they were talking about, the table began filling up with the others from their group. It was Tuesday, but the conversation was still focused on Jared's party—who was and wasn't there, who danced together, who left with who. Kia found she didn't really care. Her mind drifted off ...

"Are you going, Ki?"

"Huh?" Kia glanced up and was surprised to see Chris, from Youth Group, standing at the end of their table.

"Are you going?" he repeated. He was smiling down at her, his brown eyes soft. "To Tara's."

"To Tara's?"

"Yeah. Her cabin. For the ski weekend."

"The ski weekend?" Kia shook her head. She couldn't seem to follow any conversation today.

"Yeah. Although there won't be much skiing going on!" His eyes shone.

Kia looked puzzled. A hush fell over the table.

"I guess not," she said quietly. "I wasn't invited." She looked around, but nobody would meet her eyes. She shrugged. "I'm not much of a partier these days anyway." She climbed off the bench, acutely aware of her awkwardness, collected her lunch containers and walked away. She felt Shawna at her side a moment later.

"She just hasn't got around to asking you."

Kia kept walking. "Do you really believe that?"

"Yeah. She will."

"Maybe. Or maybe I make her uncomfortable."

"What do you mean?"

They had arrived at Kia's locker. She began to wind the dial on her lock.

"I mean she's glad it's me and not her."

"Huh?"

Kia spun around to confront Shawna. "Tara's been sleeping around for ages! She's lucked out, I'd say. She's never gotten pregnant."

Shawna picked at one of her nails.

"Okay, maybe she has," Kia continued, understanding from Shawna's expression how mistaken she'd been. "But looking at me is a reminder of ... of the abortion, I guess. Or abortions?" she asked.

Shawna didn't answer.

"I thought you and I told each other everything," Kia said softly.

"I was sworn to secrecy." Shawna looked up and pleaded with Kia. "I didn't know either, until just a few days ago. It came out when everyone was talking about you and…"

"What were they saying?"

Shawna shrugged. "They were just wondering why you hadn't had an abortion. That's when Tara told us about hers."

"Where was I when all this talking was going on?"

Shawna looked down the hall. "It was a sort of impromptu sleepover, at Rochelle's. After Jared's party."

"Sort of impromptu?"

The bell rang, signaling the start of afternoon classes, but neither Kia nor Shawna moved.

"Miss Jaswal warned me about this," Kia said finally.

"About what?"

"Nothing." Kia pulled her books out of her locker. "You better get going, Shawn, or you'll be late."

Shawna nodded but stayed put. "Maybe you're right, Kia. Maybe you do make some people feel a little uncomfortable right now. But they'll get over it once …"

Kia slammed her locker shut, turned and faced Shawna. "Once what?"

"You know what I mean."

"Yeah." Kia began walking to her next class. "They'll get over it," she said, glancing back at Shawna. "But will I?"

From: Justin <justintime@yahoo.com>
To: Kia <hazelnut@hotmail.com>
Date: March 28

Subject: T.O.Y.

hi ki & peanut,

i missed going to prenatal class last night! how soon before the 2nd set starts up?

y don't we get together and go through that binder again? we could make mon. nights our get-together night, even if prenatal is over.

hugs, uncle J

From: Justin <justintime@yahoo.com>
To: Kia <hazelnut@hotmail.com>
Date: March 29
Subject: Still T.O.Y.

hi again kia,

whatcha doing? did you get my last e-mail?

From: Justin <justintime@yahoo.com>
To: Kia <hazelnut@hotmail.com>
Date: March 30
Subject: and STILL T.O.Y.

ok kia, no one skips out of youth group without paying the price! chris says you've been at school so I know you didn't get hit by a truck or anything. if i don't hear from you soon, i'm going to come over and break your door down!

:-)   uncle J.

"I'm glad you could meet me here, Kia," Sadie said. They were walking along a trail in a park near Kia's house. "There was such a crowd at our first meeting that we couldn't really talk. But I sensed you're not overly excited about placing your baby for adoption."

"You got that right."

"Your mom and dad don't think you have any other choice, though, right?"

"Right again."

They walked in silence for a few minutes. Finally Sadie spoke again. "Have you spent much time with babies, Kia?"

"I was seven when my little sister was born. And," she added, "I play with the babies at her daycare." Although, she thought, the experience of hearing them all cry the other day had been a bit of a shock, but she wasn't going to tell Sadie that.

"Having a little sister and seeing babies at a daycare are quite different experiences than having your own baby," Sadie said. "It's not my job to try to talk you out of keeping it, but I'm wondering if you're willing to try an experiment. It's kind of a game, really."

"What is it?"

"I brought a baby for you to take care of for a week."

Kia glanced at Sadie, puzzled.

"Really, I did. Why don't you wait on that bench over there, by the pond? I'll go back to my car and get her."

"You left a baby in the car?"

Sadie smiled. "You'll see. I'll be right back."

Kia sat down and watched Sadie walk away. The reflection of the sunlight on the pond was dazzling, and Kia closed her eyes, enjoying the first truly spring-like day of the season. For a moment she forgot about Justin's rejection, adoptive parents and fair-weather friends ...

"Honk."

Kia's eyes blinked open. A Canada goose was standing

a few feet away, its head tilted, jet-black eyes studying her.

"Sorry, bud, I didn't bring any food today."

They stared at each other until Kia spotted Sadie walking back through the park. She did appear to be carrying a baby. It was wrapped in a blanket and Sadie was staring down at it, smiling. Had she really left a baby in her car?

"Congratulations, Kia," Sadie said, standing in front of her, still cradling the baby. "I'd like you to meet your little bundle of joy." There was a playful look in her eyes as she held it out to Kia.

Kia took the bundle and looked at it. "What is this?" She pulled the blanket away and found she was holding a bag of dog food. The goose craned its long neck forward to take a closer look.

"This is your newborn baby, Kia. It's a big one at ten pounds."

"This is stupid." Kia shoved the blanket and dog food at Sadie. The goose took a fluttering step back.

Sadie carefully rewrapped the bag in the blanket. "I know it seems stupid, Kia, but humor me. There's no real way of understanding the responsibilities of being a parent unless you've actually been one. All I want you to do is try it for one week. That's nothing, considering a real child will be with you for about twenty years."

Kia sighed. "What do I have to do?"

Sadie began to rock the bag of dog food. "She's crying, Kia."

Kia rolled her eyes.

Sadie heaved the package up to her shoulder and began to pat it. "Maybe she's hungry. Or she could have a wet diaper."

"Are you serious?"

"I am. I want you to choose a name for her. You need to borrow some baby clothes and also get a couple of baby bottles, soothers and some toys. You'll also need to buy enough disposable diapers to last you through the week. That will be about fifty-six."

"Fifty-six diapers?"

"Oh, yeah. You can expect to change a newborn baby at least eight times a day. And you'll need to feed it about every three hours. Each time will take about twenty minutes. So every three hours you'll need to stop whatever you're doing and feed your baby, even at night. So set your alarm to wake yourself up."

Kia shook her head. "Never mind. I get your point; babies are time-consuming. You can keep your dumb dog food. Or feed it to that goose."

"Babies are more than that, Kia," Sadie said, glancing briefly at the huge bird. "And it's one thing to know they're a big responsibility, it's another thing to actually be responsible." Sadie leaned over and gently passed the blanket-wrapped bag of dog food back to Kia. Kia took it, but she held it away from her body. "It's still crying, Kia. Try walking it."

Kia rolled her eyes again but stood up and rocked from side to side. She was aware of the goose watching her. She felt incredibly stupid.

"Your baby must always be left with a responsible adult, Kia. You can't ever leave it alone. If you go out, you must find a babysitter for it."

Kia nodded, resigned.

"And your baby will cry a few times every hour for

no apparent reason, like right now. You must hold it and rock it."

Kia began to rock a little harder, glad, at least, that this baby's nose didn't run.

"Play with your baby, Kia. Talk to it and carry it with you most of the time."

Kia nodded.

"I'll give you a ride home," Sadie said. "And don't worry. I brought a car seat for the baby. I'll lend it to you for the week."

Kia sat back down on the bench and wrapped the blanket firmly around the dog food. She didn't want anyone to get a glimpse of what she was really carrying.

"Sorry, goose," she said to the curious bird as she got up and began to follow Sadie back to the car. "I tried. I really did."

⌒

"Kia!" Angie called up the stairs.

"Yeah?" She turned the TV down.

"Someone here to see you."

"Okay," she sighed. "I'll be right there."

Kia threw back the blanket, slowly pulled herself off the couch and trudged down the stairs.

"Hi, Kia," Justin said from the doorway. "How are ya?"

"Hi, Justin." Kia's voice was expressionless.

"I told you I was going to come over and break your door down."

"You did?"

"Yeah. In my e-mail. Remember?"

"Oh," she said. "I haven't been checking my mail."

"Well, that makes me feel better," he said. "At least now I know it's not me that's the problem."

No, thought Kia. It's not you. It's everyone.

"And I guess I won't have to break your door down."

"I guess not."

"Can I come in?" he asked.

She shook her head. "I'm not allowed to have guys in the house when my parents aren't home."

Justin stepped in anyway. "I'm not just any guy. I'm your Youth Group leader. And besides," he said, glancing down at Kia's stomach and smiling, "I'll bet your parents have quit worrying about that."

"Shut up, Justin," she said. "And why are you here, anyway?"

"I'm here to help you find your lost sense of humor," he said, serious now. "And to see how you're doing." He looked her over. "The Peanut has grown since that last time I saw you two."

"I think we can quit calling her Peanut," Kia said, looking down. "She's outgrown that nickname, don't you think? And yeah, I'm more cow-like than ever."

"Cow-like? That's how you see yourself?"

"Yeah. Duh."

"C'mon, Kia. That's almost sacrilegious." He shook his head. "The creation of a baby from a mass of cells to a fully developed child in just nine months is so totally awesome. It really makes you stop and wonder about the mystery of our existence…"

"Yeah, sure, easy for you to say," she interrupted. "You're a guy. You don't have to gain twenty-five pounds in nine months." She turned and started up the stairs.

"You might as well come in. You're here anyway."

Kia picked up the TV remote from the coffee table and hit the power switch to turn it off.

"Anything good on?" Justin asked.

"No," she answered, but realized, with shock, that she couldn't even remember what she'd been watching. She'd been living in such a fog. She plunked herself down on the couch and picked up the dressed bag of dog food. Angie and her mom had found old baby clothes stored in boxes in the crawl space, and Angie had carefully dressed it in a soft green blanket sleeper with a hood. She'd even drawn a sleepy face on the bag.

Justin perched himself on the hearth across the coffee table from her. He stretched his long legs out in front of him. "What have you got there?"

"A surrogate baby."

"Really. May I hold it?"

"Gladly." Kia tossed the bag to him. "Cute, isn't she?"

"Very." Justin held the bag up to his shoulder and patted it, just as Sadie had. "Who gave it to you?"

"Sadie. This is her way of showing me what it's like to be a mother."

"Does she cry much?"

"She did the first day. But I straightened her out."

Justin looked skeptical. "How did you do that?"

"I locked her in a closet."

"Is that what Sadie had in mind?" He held her gaze.

"No." Kia tossed him an empty baby bottle. "Sadie thought I should feed it every three hours, change its diaper eight times a day and hire a babysitter for it when I'm in school."

"That's what you'd have to do if it was a real baby." Justin ignored the bottle, but he continued to hold the bag.

"But I'd love a real baby! I'd want to do all those things! This is just a stupid game. I quit after one day."

"Did you learn anything?"

"I learned that Sadie's as stupid as everyone else." Kia took a cookie out of a bag that was sitting on the couch beside her. She tossed the bag back onto the table. "Help yourself," she said.

"No thanks." Justin carefully laid the surrogate baby on the floor at his feet. "How are you feeling?"

"Fat, like I said, and I'm not even halfway there yet."

"How many weeks along are you now?"

"Eighteen." She frowned and pushed gently on one side of her swollen stomach. "And what is this? An interrogation?"

"When's your next doctor's appointment?"

"This week." She frowned again and changed her position.

"Have you gone through the adoption binder again?" he asked softly.

She nodded. "I've glanced at it."

"Any good candidates?"

She shrugged

He spoke even more quietly. "Are you really thinking of keeping your baby, Kia?"

"No. Yes. I don't know." She crossed her arms. "I'm trying to think of a way to keep her and prove that everyone is wrong. That I *can* do it."

Justin nodded.

"But I guess I know deep down," she said, "that I

can't do it alone."

They sat quietly for a minute.

"Okay," Kia said. "I'll show you the perfect couple." She got up and pulled the binder off a shelf. Justin moved over to sit on the couch beside her. She flipped through the pages until she came to the one she was looking for. "Here they are." She handed the book to him.

He read the profile, nodded and handed it back. "What is it about them that you like?"

"I think it's what I read between the lines. They say 'listening is the most important part of parenting.' That says a lot about them, don't you think?"

Justin nodded.

"And they say it's important for kids to learn to think for themselves, not to just parrot what everyone else thinks." Kia glanced at Justin. "Cool, huh?"

"Cool." He smiled.

"They don't smoke. They're environmentalists. They say they'll support their child in whatever life path he or she chooses. They sound almost too good to be true." She stared at the picture of them and then added, almost sarcastically, "The perfect parents."

"You make it sound like that's a crime."

"Only because they are and I'm not."

"You're gonna be a great parent someday, Kia."

She ignored him. "And there's one other thing I like about them."

"What's that?"

"Look at their picture again."

"They almost look like your parents."

"Yeah. Except in reverse. He's Oriental and she's

white. My baby would blend in perfectly."

"That's true. So?"

"So what?" Kia rubbed her stomach, frowning again.

"Shall we call Sadie? Get her to set up a meeting?"

"What's the rush?"

"C'mon, Kia," Justin said quietly. "You said yourself this couple looks almost too good to be true. It's time to meet them."

"All right. I'll phone her. Later. Something's happening in here." She rubbed her stomach again.

"Are you okay?"

"Yeah, it doesn't hurt. But, it feels weird."

"Maybe we should call your doctor."

"No, it's not that bad, it's just …"

"What?" Justin sounded alarmed.

Kia sat up straight. Her eyes lit up when she turned to him. "It's moving! I've been wondering what that weird feeling was!"

"Cool." Justin leaned forward. "Do you think I can feel it too?"

"I don't know. It's just a fluttering sensation, really. Here. Give me your hand." She placed his hand on one side of her stomach and pressed on it with both her own. They sat still for a moment. "There! Did you feel that?"

"I felt a kind of gurgle. That was the baby?"

"Yeah. I think so."

"Wow."

Kia kept Justin's warm hand pressed against her side long after the fluttering had stopped. Their breathing seemed to be in perfect unison; she could feel his warm breath on her cheek. He didn't seem in any hurry to pull his hand away. Finally, though, she sat back. "I guess she's gone to sleep."

Justin stood up and moved back to the hearth. "You gonna be okay?" he asked.

"Yeah."

"You'll check your e-mail?"

She smiled. "Maybe."

"And you'll come back to Youth Group?"

"Are you bringing popcorn next time?"

"Popcorn and, as a special treat, pickles."

"Then I'll come."

"Good. And you'll phone Sadie?"

"Yeah. Just to get you off my back."

Justin picked up the bag of dog food and handed it to Kia. "Take care of her, Ki. It breaks my heart to think she's being neglected."

"The week's almost up. I'm going to feed her to the neighbor's dog."

Justin feigned horror. "Oh, Kia. No!"

"Yes."

"Then she's coming with me." Justin snatched the bag back and wrapped it more securely in the blanket as he went down the stairs.

"I don't think Sadie will approve of me giving her away," Kia laughed, but then realized what she'd said. "Actually," she added, serious now, "I guess that's the whole point. Take her."

"Better to give her to me than to put her in a closet."

"You're right." She rubbed the side of her stomach. "There she goes again." She glanced at Justin's bundle. "You can have that baby. I've got my own."

~ taste buds have formed inside the mouth and on the tongue
~ loud noises on the outside may startle the baby
~ weighs about one pound

April 4

Dear Peanut (I have to think of another name for you),

Feeling you move is too amazing! I can't believe I have a little person inside of me who I've never met. It almost seems like you're an alien! But keep moving, it's so awesome.

I wish I could read Justin's mind. He seems as fascinated by all this as I am. Is it me that turns him off? My age? Or is it just because I'm in the Youth Group? What did he mean when he said that there is something I don't understand?

Kia pushed Grace's wheelchair into a sunny corner of the room and then brought her a cup of tea.

"So Kia," Grace said, after taking a sip, "I didn't expect to see you again until your next piano performance on Wednesday."

"I just felt like a visit," Kia said. "A week is too long. Besides, you're my favorite friend right now."

"I'm happy to see you too, Kia," Grace said, but she

looked puzzled. They sat quietly while Grace struggled to get her teacup to her mouth. She took another sip and then continued. "So why don't you get right to the point and tell me what's wrong?"

Kia feigned surprise. "What makes you think something's wrong?"

"Just that intuition thing again, I guess." Grace shrugged.

Kia stared out at the turbulent river. The leaves were beginning to reappear on the trees and they cast interesting shadows on the wide expanse of lawn. "So haven't you noticed anything different about me, Grace?" she asked finally, turning to look directly at the old woman.

Grace's teacup clattered as she dropped it back on the saucer. She sat back in her wheelchair. "Yes Kia, I can see you're pregnant. I'm old, but I'm not blind."

"Then why haven't you said anything?"

"I knew you would talk about it when you were ready."

"I wanted to talk about it ... but it's a hard thing to ... to bring up." Kia glanced around the room. "What does everyone else think about it?" she asked quietly. "Are they all shocked? Disgusted?"

"I don't know if anyone else has even noticed," Grace answered. "They don't spend as much time with you as I do." She leaned forward, frowning. "And don't tell me the reaction of these old people is your biggest problem right now!"

Kia heard the teasing in Grace's voice. "No, not the biggest, but one of them."

"Then rest assured, Kia," Grace said, placing her hand

on Kia's arm, "the people here have been around way too long to be shocked by something like this. So, why don't you tell me what else is bothering you?"

Kia looked at Grace, and then back out the window. "Have you got all day? There's so much, I don't even know where to start."

"I've got nothing but time, Kia, you know that. Start at the beginning. Is the father that young man you were telling me about awhile back? The one who ...?"

"Yep. He's the one." Kia told Grace about the near-abortion and how angry Derek was with her for not going through with it.

"Okay, now I know about Derek," Grace said when Kia was finished. "What else is going on?"

Kia picked up her teacup and studied the bottom of it. "I don't even know where to start," she said. "There's my friends, if you can still call them that ..."

"What's happening with your friends?"

"Nothing! That's the problem. They don't call me. We used to chat on the computer all the time..."

"Chat on the computer?"

"Yeah." Kia tried to think of a way to explain it. "It's like sending notes to each other, but over the computer. I send a note to Shawna and it shows up on her computer screen. She sends one back. Kind of like talking on the phone, but you can send notes to a bunch of people at the same time."

"Interesting. You'll have to show me how to do that."

Kia nodded absently. "I will. But right now they're not sending me anything, except Shawna, and even she seems ... distant."

"Why do you think that is?"

"I don't know. I guess it's because I'm not doing the same things as them anymore. I'm not playing baseball. or going to parties or shopping or any of that stuff."

"You're busy growing a baby."

"Yeah. And they're not into that."

Grace nodded.

"But they could at least pretend to be interested in what's happening to me."

"Do you think it scares them?"

Kia shrugged. "I don't know. Kelsey told Shawna that she's not even allowed to hang out with me!"

Grace struggled with her teacup again.

"I guess her parents think that she might start having sex too if she hangs out with me," Kia said bitterly.

"That could be it, I guess. Or perhaps seeing you reminds Kelsey's parents of what they don't want to think about."

"And what's that?"

"That their daughter is growing up too. Given different circumstances, it could be Kelsey that was having a baby."

"It's stupid. Everyone, even complete strangers, looks at my stomach and not in my eyes anymore."

They sat quietly for a few minutes.

"I can't figure out why *I* got pregnant in the first place, and not someone more deserving …"

"More deserving? Like someone who is trying to get pregnant?"

"Yeah, or someone too stupid to use birth control."

Grace nodded. "Go on. What else is bothering you?"

Kia slumped lower in the chair. "I have to decide what to do with the baby after it's born."

Grace nodded. "That's a tough one."

"You can say that again."

"Are you close to making a decision?"

"I really really want to keep it." Kia hugged her stomach. "It's so much a part of me. I can't imagine giving it away."

"But?"

Kia sighed. "I know how hard it is to be a single parent, especially when you're only seventeen. I don't want to give up all the stuff I do and have..."

"Being a parent certainly ties you down."

"I know. I had a pretend baby for a week and even that was too much for me." Kia watched as a squirrel scampered across the lawn toward the building. It seemed to be looking at them through the window. "And I didn't even take care of it!"

"Justin brings peanuts and feeds them," Grace said, distracted by the squirrel. She glanced up at the wall clock. "Usually about this time. I wonder where he is?"

That reminded Kia. "If only I had a partner. Someone to raise the baby with. You know anyone who would want the job, Grace?" she teased.

"Oh, look," Grace said, raising a stiff arm and pointing to a tall, slim figure coming along the grass, tossing peanuts out of a paper bag. "There he is now."

Kia noticed that many of the other seniors were moving toward the window to watch the activity outside. "And look, he's brought Blair with him."

Kia watched as another young man came up along-

side Justin with his own bag of peanuts. He was stockier
and athletic looking. The two of them waved cheerfully
at the room full of seniors, and then started encouraging
the squirrels to get closer to them, even to eat out of
their hands.

"Who is Blair?" Kia asked.

Grace dragged her eyes away from the scene on the
lawn to look at Kia. "Blair? Why, Blair is Justin's ..." She
paused and her eyes became more focused. "His friend,"
she said finally. "And such a nice young man too."

She went back to watching the squirrels. Justin and
Blair had even taught them some tricks, like climbing
right up their bodies to retrieve peanuts off their shoulders. The seniors clapped in appreciation.

"It's amazing that they never get scratched or bit-
ten," Grace commented.

Kia watched, but she didn't see. She was overcome
by a sinking sensation that had started deep in her stomach and radiated to every part of her body.

Finally, Grace turned back to Kia. "So, where were
we?" she asked, smiling kindly.

Kia kept her eyes on the two figures outside. "I don't
remember," she said, trying to drag herself back to the
present.

"I think," Grace squinted, "we were talking about
what you were going to do with the baby."

Kia nodded.

"Oh," Grace said, sitting up. "You mentioned that
you were looking for a partner, and wanted to know if I
knew one."

Kia met Grace's eyes and nodded. "Yeah," she said.

"But that possibility seems less likely all the time."

Grace nodded sadly. "Yes, I guess it is a little late in the game for that."

"I guess," Kia said, and her eyes moved back to the two young men who were having such a good time feeding the squirrels.

⁓

Kia passed the picture from the ultrasound around the circle at check-in. This time she got the response she was looking for.

"This is so cool, Kia," Laurel said. "Aren't you, like, dying to hold her?"

Kia smiled. "It's weird. Here I am carrying a little person around inside me but I've never even met her. I so want to know what she looks like. I wish I could just unzip my stomach, pull her out, take a good look at her and then pop her back in."

Justin laughed. "Yeah, too bad zippers hadn't been invented when women were created."

"Can you actually tell it's a girl?" Chris asked.

Kia shook her head.

"Sure you can," Mike said, taking the picture from Meagan. "If there's a UDT floating around…"

"A what?" Kia asked.

"An unidentified dangly thingie."

Kia laughed. "There's nothing like that. Must be a girl after all."

"I'll tell you," Mike said. He squinted at the photo. "Hmm, it just looks like a bunch of gray and black blobs to me."

Meagan snatched it out of his hand. "That's because you're blind," she said, holding it out in front of him. "Look, here's its bum, here's the head," she said, pointing to the picture. "And here are the arms and legs. Do you see it now?"

Mike shook his head. "Sorry."

Meagan passed it on. "It's crystal clear. I don't know what your problem is."

"You," Mike said, gently punching her arm. "Are you done, Kia? Is it my turn?"

She nodded. "That's it."

"Well," he said, "I've got some really sad news. A guy in my grade killed himself on the weekend. Slashed his wrists."

The room grew still.

"I didn't know him all that well. By the time I got to school this morning a bunch of kids had already set up a huge memorial around his locker. They had a poster-sized picture of him taped on it, and all kinds of his stuff lying around. Flowers and wreaths filled the whole hallway."

"Did he leave a note?" Justin asked quietly.

"Yeah, for his parents. He said he couldn't handle the harassment anymore, although everyone swore he acted like it never bothered him."

"Yeah, well, duh. Who ever admits that they're bugged? You'd just get it twice as bad," Meagan commented.

"And you know," Mike continued, "for a guy who didn't think he had any friends, there was sure a lot of kids hanging around his locker crying."

"Even the guys who bullied him?" Laurel asked.

Mike nodded. "A lot of them."

"What was he being harassed about?" Justin asked. Kia was shocked to see how pale he'd become.

"Everyone called him fag, queer, homo."

"Was he?" Chris asked.

Justin turned to Chris before Mike could answer, his voice steely. "So what if he was?" he asked. "Does that make him any less of a person than anyone else?"

"I didn't mean it that way," Chris answered, defensively. "I just asked if he was."

The room grew silent again. Kia knew everyone was as shocked as she was at Justin's reaction. They'd never heard him speak to anyone the way he'd just spoken to Chris.

"Sorry, Chris," Justin said after a long moment. "I overreacted."

"That's okay," Chris mumbled.

"But try to imagine," Justin went on, "how horrible a person must feel before they actually consider death preferable to life." Kia could see that Justin's hands were trembling. He rubbed his face.

She reached out and rubbed his back. "It's okay," she said.

He shook his head. "No, it's not. Another kid is dead."

"You're right," she said, dropping her hand.

He looked down at her. "But thanks anyway."

She met his eyes and nodded. They sat quietly for another minute.

"Has everyone checked in, then?" Justin asked, looking around the circle.

The pensive group nodded together.

"Then I'd like to suggest we break for something to eat," he said. He turned to Kia. "I brought the pickles," he said quietly.

"Good," she smiled. "The peanut's getting hungry." She looked around at the puzzled expressions. "Snack time," she announced, glad to break the solemn mood. "Popcorn for you guys, and pickles for us," she said, rubbing her stomach.

April 7
Today I turn 17.

I remember turning 16. That seems like 20 years ago. Never in a trillion years would I have guessed that my life could change so much so quickly. (And all because of one night!) And what will I be doing one year from today?

The word 'birthday' means so much more this year. It's not just a day to eat cake and open presents. I am now responsible for another person's birthday. That will be the first day of a new life. Or is it? The little person inside me is alive already …

Birth. Only five letters but such a huge moment. Going from life in the womb to life on the outside. Life on the inside is so much safer. So much can go wrong on the outside. Babies are dependent on the decisions — good or bad — of the people in their life. Decisions …

A very small part of me would like to go back to being an innocent newborn. Where someone else would have to decide …

From: Justin <justintime@yahoo.com>
To: Kia <hazelnut@hotmail.com>
Date: April 8
Subject: interview

hi kia, a little bird told me u r interviewing some adoptive
parents. do u need someone (like me!) along for moral
support?

TOY,
Justin

From: Kia <hazelnut@hotmail.com>
To: Justin <justintime@yahoo.com>
Date: April 8
Subject: Re: interview

hi justin, ya, i've got my meeting with Sadie fri. nite. then we
meet with joanna & brett (the perfect parents) on sat. i'd
luv to have you there if you can make it.

kia & the pumpkin

From: Justin <justintime@yahoo.com>
To: Kia <hazelnut@hotmail.com>
Date: April 8
Subject: the pumpkin!!

i liked 'peanut' better. (and peanut butter!) pumpkins make
me think of scary faces.

DARN! i have to work fri. nite. i'm taking my seniors to the
theatre — can't miss that — but i'll be there on sat. what
time? e-mail me fri. nite and tell me how it goes with sadie.

hugs
uncle J

From: Kia <hazelnut@hotmail.com>

To: Justin <justintime@yahoo.com>

Date: April 11

Subject: tomorrow

hi justin, how was the theatre? did our seniors behave themselves? :-)

the meeting with sadie was weird. we talked about the questions i should ask them and what to expect they'll ask me, but then she told me about some of the fears THEY might be having. i never thought about them having fears! sadie said it was normal for me to feel jealous of them and 2 worry that they won't like me or the baby! believe me, i'm not worried about that — my baby is going to be so perfect. the perfect baby for the perfect parents. (gag.) i'm so nervous about tomorrow. thanks for coming with me. we're supposed to be there @ 10:00.

k & c (c for coconut, cuz that's the biggest nut I can think of. happy now?)

HALFWAY THERE!
~ Baby has asleep and awake patterns similar to a newborn
~ Female baby has developed a uterus
~ Rapid growth period slows down

April 11
What will be worse?
Liking them and having no reason NOT to give her up?
Or not liking them and having to choose again?

"You need to eat, Ki."

"I'll eat after. I'm way too nervous."

Kia sat with her father and Angie at the kitchen table. The sound of her dad's fingers drumming on the table matched the sound of the rain dripping from the overflowing gutters.

"Can I have your strawberries then?" Angie asked.

Kia pushed her bowl toward her sister. "They're all yours," she said.

Kia's father cleared his throat. "We'd really like to come with you, Kia," he said again. "I think it's important that we decide this thing together."

"This is not a thing," Kia said. She slumped in her chair and folded her arms across her chest. They'd been through it all the night before, but she sensed they were going to have to discuss it again this morning. She glanced at her watch. Forty-five more minutes before Justin would arrive.

"It's just that we're older, honey. And the older you get, the better judge of character you become."

"I'm a good judge of character."

"Is that right?"

"Yes, it is." She noticed her father's skeptical expression. "What?"

"I don't think you are."

"Why do you say that?"

"Think about it."

Kia studied him. She didn't know what he was talking about.

"How about Derek?" he reminded her. "You admitted yourself that you misjudged his character."

"That's different." She felt her face flush.

"Why?"

"It just is." She wasn't going to explain to him that her mistake with Derek wasn't so much that she'd misjudged him. It was that she'd allowed herself to give in to the rush of desire she experienced every time they were together. She realized now that she'd never even taken the time to get to know his character.

"It's just that this is not the kind of decision a girl your age should be making," her dad continued. "Your mom and I have raised children, we can see through idealistic platitudes to the real character traits that matter."

"Like what, Dad?" Kia asked, unconvinced.

"Well, like ..." He paused, unable to name anything.

"I'm not going to choose a couple of idiots to give my baby to, Dad. This matters a lot to me."

"It just seems you're already so set on this one couple. You should interview lots of people."

"I will if these guys aren't perfect."

"Nobody's perfect, Kia." Her dad sighed.

"I am," Angie said, grinning as she carried her bowl to the sink.

Kia smiled at her little sister, grateful for the interruption.

"Aside from you," Kia's dad said, also smiling.

Kia glanced from her father to Angie and realized, again, that the family dynamics were shifting. The roles they'd all played for so many years had changed. But even with her bulging stomach, the hardest shift of all was for her father to accept that she was no longer just a girl. She was a young adult who had some big decisions ahead of her. And she would make them herself.

∽

Kia felt Justin's arm slide around her shoulders when Brett and Joanna arrived at Sadie's office. Kia studied the couple carefully. Her first thought was that they looked older than they did in the picture. They both shook hands with her, and when Kia looked into Joanna's eyes, their beauty startled her. It wasn't the heavily made-up glossy-magazine kind of beauty, but the beauty of a wise, warm and caring woman. Brett's handshake was firm and his smile friendly. Justin shook their hands too, and Sadie introduced him as Kia's friend, pointedly adding that he was not the father of the baby.

"So," Brett said once they were all seated. "Are you as nervous as we are?"

Kia laughed at the unexpected question. "Yes," she admitted. "I couldn't eat anything this morning."

"Me neither," Joanna said. "And I didn't sleep a wink last night."

"I thought we were going to be late for this meeting," Brett said, "because Joanna kept changing her mind about what to wear."

Kia smiled as Joanna gave her husband a friendly swat. "Casual, but not too casual," he teased, putting his arm around his wife's chair. "Fashionable, but not trendy. It's hard to know what look a wannabe adoptive mother should have."

"I wish I had that problem," Kia said, smiling at Brett. "I don't have much to choose from right now." She put her hands on her stomach.

"Have you felt it move yet?" Joanna asked.

"Yeah, she's been kicking like crazy all morning. I think she knows how nervous I am. My adrenaline must be pumping through her too."

"Her?" Brett asked. "Do you know it's a girl?"

"No," Kia admitted. She pulled the ultrasound photo out of her purse. "I just have a strong feeling about it. Here's her first photo."

Joanna took the photo from Kia and studied it. She handed it to Brett. "It's miraculous, isn't it?" she commented quietly. Brett peered at the photo and nodded. He handed it back to Kia and then picked up his wife's hand.

"Do you care what it is?" Kia asked.

They shook their heads.

"So, I know you each have questions prepared," Sadie said, speaking for the first time since the meeting began. "Do you want to take turns, or ...?"

Kia glanced at Joanna and Brett, they looked back at her. They all shrugged and turned to Sadie for guidance.

"Well then, Kia, why don't you get the ball rolling? What would you like to ask Joanna and Brett?"

"Well ..." She hesitated. There was only one thing she really wanted to know. "You said in the adoption profile something about the birth mom being a special part of your lives. Can you tell me what you mean by that?"

Joanna spoke first. She leaned forward. "If you choose us as the adoptive parents, Kia," she said quietly, "we would decide together what kind of an arrangement would work best for everyone. It could mean that you would visit us and get to know the child, or another option would be that we would send you pictures and letters. I expect each birth parent has different ideas about how much involvement they want. But we're open to almost any arrangement."

"Our adopted child will always know that she has a birth mom who loves her as much as we do," Brett said, smiling. "She'll be luckier than all those kids who only have two parents."

Kia nodded, her eyes shining. "Thanks."

"Your turn to ask Kia a question," Sadie said to Brett and Joanna.

"I hate to pry," Joanna said, "but I'm wondering what you can tell us about the birth father. Will he also want to stay connected with the baby?"

Kia felt her energy drain. They'd started with the

hardest question of all. But then she felt Justin's hand squeeze her shoulder and it gave her the encouragement she needed. "Derek and I aren't even talking. We only went out for awhile and I got pregnant the only time we ever ... did it," she said quietly. "He wanted me to abort it and he's angry that I didn't." Kia took a deep breath and let it out slowly. "I don't think he'll want anything to do with the baby, but I guess I'll have to talk to him about it eventually."

Joanna nodded, looking sympathetic. "Life is strange, isn't it? Here I am, desperately trying to get pregnant, and you ... well, you know what I mean."

Kia nodded. "Yeah, I do." She sat quietly for a moment. "Okay, my turn to ask you a question."

"Shoot," Brett said.

"What scares you the most about all this?"

Brett and Joanna looked at each other and laughed. "You ask tough questions, Kia," Joanna said.

"You're not scared of anything?" Kia asked.

"No, that's not it," Joanna said. "There are so many things I'm scared of I don't know where to start!"

"Just name a few," Kia suggested.

"Well," Joanna said, looking at Brett, "I guess the biggie is that you'll choose us to be the adoptive parents, we'll get our hopes up, and then you'll change your mind at the last minute." She added quietly, "It happened once before."

Kia watched as Brett gently rubbed her back.

"What else?" Kia asked.

"That you won't choose us to be the parents," Joanna said.

"Anything else?" Kia asked.

"I've got one," Brett said. "You'll choose us, we'll take the baby home, you'll come visit us and decide you just can't leave her, and you'll take her away." Kia could see the pain in Brett's dark eyes as he described the scenario. "And I've been worried that you might be doing drugs and messing it up," he added, "but I can see now that that's not likely."

Kia shook her head.

"Wow," Sadie said, breaking into the conversation. "I really admire your honesty."

"Yeah, really," Justin said.

Joanna looked at Justin, almost as if noticing him for the first time. "You two are just friends?"

Kia and Justin nodded, looking at each other.

"So there's no chance you're suddenly going to decide to raise this baby together?"

"No chance," Justin said quietly, still looking at Kia. But this time she didn't return his gaze.

"Okay," Sadie said, changing the subject. "Whose turn is it to ask a question?"

"I think it's mine," Kia said, clearing her throat.

Joanna nodded encouragingly.

"What if my baby is born and there is something wrong with it? Like it's got Down's syndrome or something? Would you still want to adopt it?"

There was no hesitation. They nodded in unison. "Do you have some reason to believe there might be something wrong?" Sadie asked.

"No, but you never know." Kia placed her hand on her stomach. "There she goes again."

"The baby?" Joanna asked.

"Uh-huh. I'm sure she's got all her limbs. And then some."

"May I feel?"

"Sure."

Justin and Joanna exchanged seats, and Joanna put her hand on Kia's stomach.

"Oh!" Joanna sat up straight, eyes wide.

"That was her," Kia said. She moved Joanna's hand a little, placing it closer to where Joanna would feel the baby's movements.

"That is so awesome."

Kia could hear reverence in Joanna's voice. They studied each other while they waited for another movement. Again, Kia was struck by the depth of character she saw in Joanna's face. Her dad was wrong. She could judge people accurately, and she knew that Joanna and Brett would make great parents.

If only she was as sure she could give them her baby.

~

April 14

I feel like I have a split personality and both of me are having a big fight inside my head. I can't stand it. It goes like this —

Me #1 — They're perfect. Brett's cool. Joanna's wonderful.

Me #2 — But this is our baby. Giving it away — even to THE PERFECT PARENTS — will be like giving away an arm, a leg, even our heart!

Me #1 – But we'll be able to go visit. She'll know we are her birth mom.

Me #2 – Maybe she'll know she is our flesh and blood but her real mom will be Joanna. Joanna will be the one rocking her to sleep, kissing her scrapes and bruises, reading her bedtime stories …

Me #1 – Quit being so romantic! Joanna will also be changing stinky diapers, getting up in the middle of the night and listening to her whine. We'll just get to enjoy her.

Me #2 – My baby won't whine.

Me #1- Get a life.

Me #2 – I can't give her away. Even to THE PERFECT PARENTS.

Me #1 – Yes you can. And you will.

Me #2 – Not if I can help it.

Me #1 – I've got our parents, Justin <u>and</u> Sadie on my side. Now I've got Brett and Joanna too, as well as every other living person we know!

Me #2 – Yeah, but …

Me #1 – But what?

Me #2 – I've always had more pull than you.

Me #1 – LOL. We'll see, now, won't we?

Me #2 – (deep sigh) Yes, I guess we will.

⌒

Kia's heart sank when she heard the familiar thumping of the car's boom box. It was a Saturday afternoon and she and Justin were watching her former team play baseball. Neither she nor Derek had ever discussed the confrontation they'd had at Jared's party, and they'd successfully managed to avoid each other … until now.

"Oh, no," she groaned.

"What is it?" Justin asked, concerned.

"Derek's here," she said, glancing over at the parking lot and confirming her suspicions. "Let's go." She began to stand up.

"Are you going to spend the rest of your life running away from your problems, Kia?"

"Just this one. C'mon."

But Justin didn't budge. He turned back to the ball game.

Kia sighed and sat back down. "This could get ugly."

Justin put his arm around her shoulder and she leaned into him. She concentrated on the game, hoping Derek wouldn't notice her here. He didn't. Not for the first fifteen minutes, anyway. Kia was aware that he was standing with his friends, over to her right, near the first-base line. Some of the players were also aware of it, she noticed. The way they ran the bases changed subtly. It was less assertive and more self-conscious. There were furtive glances at the boys, and then a toss of the hair. The girls on the bench feigned disinterest, but the total concentration on the game was gone. Samantha, on first base, preened herself. She pulled the elastic out of her hair, smoothed it all back with her fingers and then wrapped the elastic around it again. She tugged down on her shorts after retieing her shoes.

Kia glanced at Justin and saw he was watching Samantha too. He smiled. "Makes you think of the mating dance of an exotic bird, doesn't it?" he asked.

She nodded. " And to think I was once part of that dance."

"And you will be again."

Kia thought about that. Would she? Now that she'd viewed it from the outside, would she ever be so … innocent again?

The boys eventually grew restless and began to make their way over to the concession building. They had to walk past the spectator stands where Kia sat with Justin. For a moment she thought Derek was going to walk right past them without looking up, but then she saw one of the other boys elbow him in the ribs and nod in her direction. Derek looked up and they made eye contact. He slowed down, glanced at Justin, down at her stomach, then back to her eyes. She refused to look away. She felt her heart pattering in her chest. The baby gave a hard kick. Derek kept staring at her. She refused to be intimidated. Finally, he shook his head, as if dismissing her as not worth the effort, then turned and caught up with the others.

"There. That wasn't so bad, was it?" Justin asked. He took his arm off her shoulder.

She took a deep breath and let it out slowly. She felt the beating of her heart slowly return to normal.

"And I don't know what you saw in him," Justin teased. "Couldn't be those broad shoulders, that skinny waist, those long legs, could it? How about that drop-dead gorgeous face? You really know how to pick 'em."

"Are you calling me shallow?" she asked, but she had to laugh. Even now, with the ambivalent feelings she had for Derek, she couldn't help noticing all those things again. But the cool blue gaze had cured her. There was nothing she liked about those eyes anymore.

She found those blue eyes fixed on her again on

Monday morning at school. It was her study block and she was reading in the cafeteria, which doubled as a study hall. He plunked himself down across the table from her. He stretched his long legs out, placed his elbows on the table and propped his head on his hands.

"Well, Kia, you've got way more guts than I gave you credit for."

"What are you talking about?" She glared at him, forcing herself to see past the arrogance to the frightened boy he'd become at Jared's party.

"Walkin' around, looking like that." He glanced at her stomach.

She shrugged and pretended to read again.

"Any regrets?" he asked, smugly.

She put her book down. It didn't look like he was going to leave any time soon. "Only one. Getting pregnant."

"Yeah," he grinned, "but I bet you don't regret the part that got you that way."

It was her turn to dismiss him. She shook her head and picked up her book again, but then put it back down. "You know, being pregnant has taught me a lot."

"Like what?"

"Like who my friends are."

"And who are they?" he asked, his voice dripping with sarcasm. "That faggot you were at the park with?"

She cringed at the word. That was what Derek called anyone he didn't like. "Yeah, like him. And the kids in my youth group. Shawna's the only one around here who occasionally talks to me or includes me in anything anymore. I think everyone else thinks pregnancy is … a disease. Something they might catch."

He sat back and folded his arms across his chest. "What are you going to do with it?"

"The baby?"

"No, the faggot. What do ya think?"

Kia ignored him. "I might put it up for adoption. Which reminds me. I interviewed a couple who'd like to adopt it, but they want to know if you're going to be a problem."

"What kind of problem?"

"Like if you're going to claim the baby for yourself. Or start pestering them for visiting rights or something."

Derek glanced about, making sure Kia hadn't been overheard. "Tell 'em not to worry about that. I don't even know if it is my baby."

Kia shook her head. "That's another thing I've learned. If I hadn't got pregnant I might still be going out with pricks like you."

"Oh, so now you go out with fags? That's a safe bet. But how are you going to feel when you get dumped for another guy?"

"I'm not going out with Justin, if that's who you're talkin' about." She was going to add, "and he's not gay," but she didn't. The bell rang, signaling the end of the period, so Kia began to collect her things. Derek didn't move. She glanced at him. He remained sitting very still, watching her. She couldn't read his expression, but she noticed the sneer was gone.

"What?" she asked.

"Nothing," he said quietly, then stood to leave. "It's just weird, you know, to think…" He glanced down at her stomach and then back to her eyes. Suddenly she remembered why she had fallen so hard for him.

"Yeah," she said. "I know." She held his eyes in her own, a million unspoken thoughts hanging in the air between them. Finally he looked away, and they left the cafeteria together.

From: Kia <hazelnut@hotmail.com>
To: Justin <justintime@yahoo.com>
Date: May 2
Subject: fat clothes

hi justin, i got a call from joanna today. she wants to know if she can buy me some more fat clothes. should i let her? do u think it's bribery? will I be committing myself if i let her?

W B ASAP
k.

Justin didn't write back. Instead, he showed up at Kia's door early that evening and invited her to go for a walk. She grabbed a jacket and they strolled down the street toward the same park that Kia had gone to with Sadie.

"Have you decided to let Joanna buy you clothes?" he asked.

"No, I can't decide. What do you think?"

"I don't think it's bribery. She just genuinely wants to help, but it'll probably make you feel a sense of obligation."

"Yeah, I know."

They walked along in comfortable silence until they came to the pond, where they settled themselves on a bench.

"I'm surprised you're still undecided," Justin said finally. "I don't think you'll find a better couple than Joanna and Brett."

"I know. I'm not even going to interview anyone else." Kia watched as a turtle pulled itself up out of the water and onto a rock, where it stretched its neck out, soaking up the last bit of warmth from the day's sunlight. "It's just that I'm not sure I'll be able to hand her over." She hugged her stomach protectively. "And I don't want them to have to go through that again." Kia heard Justin sigh. "And," she added quietly, "I still haven't given up hope of finding a partner to help me raise her."

"Kia …"

"I know."

"What do you know?"

"That you don't think I'm going to find a partner." Kia rubbed the side of her stomach.

"Is it kicking?" Justin asked, his eyes lighting up.

"Yeah. Here." She took his hand and placed it on her stomach.

"Whoa! What was that?"

"I think it must be her heel or … something sharp. Maybe an elbow."

"Doesn't it hurt?" Justin asked, his wide hand still stretched across her stomach.

"No, not really. But it gets a little uncomfortable."

"I guess."

They sat quietly for a moment, feeling the baby's movements.

"Who's Blair, Justin?" Kia asked.

Justin tensed—very slightly, but Kia could feel it in

his hand that rested on her stomach.

"A friend. A good friend," he answered. "Why?"

"Just wondering. I saw you with him when you were feeding squirrels at the seniors' home."

Justin nodded. He took his hand off her stomach and sat back on the bench.

"How come you never talk about your private life?" she asked. "I really don't know anything about you."

"I guess that's why it's called a *private* life," he answered.

"But you know everything about me."

"Okay, Kia," he said. "What do you want to know?"

"Do you have a girlfriend?"

"No, I don't."

"Have you ever had one?"

Justin nodded. "I dated a girl a few times in high school. She was really nice, but ..." Justin looked down at her. "What are you getting at, Kia?" he asked quietly.

"Derek called you a fag today. He calls lots of people that, but ..."

Justin took a deep breath and then exhaled slowly. "I am gay, Kia," he said solemnly, "if that's what you want to know."

She stared at him, then her eyes narrowed. "Nice try, Justin, but I don't believe you." She tried to laugh, but he continued to regard her seriously. "You're kidding, right?"

He shook his head.

She slid away from him on the bench. "You're always watching out for me and touching me and ... I don't believe this. I know you've got feelings for me."

"I do. You're right." He rubbed his face wearily.

"So what are you talking about?"

He shook his head and stared at the pond. "It's confusing. I am attracted to you, but generally I'm more attracted to guys."

She stared at his profile, as if seeing him for the first time.

"It's not that unusual, Kia." He turned back to her. "Don't you remember that from your sexuality classes? People's preferences can range from completely straight or gay to somewhere in between." He watched as she turned away. He reached out to touch her but hesitated. He put his hand back in his lap. "I've just recently come out. Not too many people know, but a few do. I'm finding it really hard to talk about."

"Blair is …?"

Justin laughed, just a little. "Blair is still my friend. I want more, but he doesn't want to be …" He paused and then added, with emphasis, "tied down." He sighed. "Sound familiar?"

Kia didn't respond.

"You know," he continued, "I thought I'd finally come to terms with being gay, but going with you to your prenatal classes and seeing your baby on the ultrasound and watching your stomach grow and thinking about being a parent …" He stopped and caught his breath. "That's all affected me somehow. We're taught, from the time we're little, that we'll grow up, get married, have babies …" He paused. "It's hard for me to accept that I'm not going to have that life. I liked the fantasy. It was safe. And …" He paused, looking for the right words. "I guess that's why I didn't tell you sooner."

"You can still have it!" Kia hated the desperation she heard in her voice. "With me."

He smiled wistfully, shaking his head. "Your sexual orientation is not something you can change, Kia, just because you wish for it. But even if I was straight," he said, "I still couldn't be your partner."

"Why not? You said you have feelings for me."

"You're so young, Kia, and you're in my Youth Group …"

"I'm mature for my age," she said, cutting him off. "You said so yourself. And I could quit Youth Group and …"

"It makes no difference anyway, Ki," Justin said firmly. "I am gay. Someday you're going to meet the right guy and fall in love. You might choose to get married or you might not. But you'll be able to have more children."

"I don't want more children," she said, crossing her arms stubbornly. "I want this one. And I wish you'd told me this before."

Justin ran both hands through his hair and looked away. "I'm sorry, Kia. I thought you must at least suspect." He swallowed hard. "And it's still not an easy thing for me to talk about."

"Does the rest of the youth group know?"

Justin shrugged. "I'm not sure. And it's not really their business anyway. The Rev does," he added. "He's the one who talked me into coming out. But it's a slow process."

Kia dropped her head, her long hair falling over her face. It felt like something had died inside her. Hope, perhaps.

They sat quietly for a long time. Finally Kia spoke again. "You'd have made such a good father too."

"I hope I still can be a father someday, but if not, maybe I really could be an uncle to your future kids."

She moved closer to him, picked up his hand and placed it on the side of her stomach again. "Did you feel that?" she asked, her eyes bright.

"Yeah."

"She wanted you to be her father too."

He smiled, sadly.

"We could still raise her together."

"You know, I actually gave that some thought, but then I realized how unfair that would be to her, the baby. One of us would fall in love with someone else and would need to leave this relationship. She wouldn't understand."

Kia didn't respond.

Justin picked up a long strand of her hair and twisted it between his fingers, feeling its texture. "Some guy is going to be so lucky …"

She looked up, her eyes shimmering with tears. "I hope it works out with Blair. He looks like a nice guy."

He smiled, untangled his fingers from her hair and wrapped his arms around her. They hugged for a long time, feeling the depth of their friendship.

◡

May 3
I have to give her up.
There.
I've said it.

the third trimester

"That's a strong heartbeat your baby has, Kia." Dr. Miyata jotted something in the file.

"She's not *my* baby anymore." Kia struggled to a sitting position. By now she knew that the heart-rate check was the last thing the doctor did each time.

"It is *your* baby, Kia," the doctor said as she put the file aside and sat beside the examining table, "until you give it away. And *it* is depending on *you* to provide a nourishing and healthy prenatal environment. That's an extremely important parental responsibility." She studied Kia carefully. "And you will always be this child's birth mother. Nobody can take that away from you."

"Being a birth mom means nothing. It means I got pregnant. Just about any female can do that."

"The woman you're giving her to couldn't."

Kia just shrugged.

"And not every child is lucky enough to be given to carefully screened and selected parents. Ask any social worker or schoolteacher. Some kids are real unlucky with the parents they get. And those are their biological ones."

Kia slid off the examination table and zipped up the fasteners on her maternity pants. "I haven't got much more room to grow in these," she commented.

"Maybe you could wear dresses for the summer," the doctor suggested.

"You mean tents. Or moo-moos. Oh yeah. They're flattering."

The doctor ignored the comment. "You'll probably find them cooler in the heat, anyway." She watched as Kia sat in the chair and leaned over her bulging belly to tie up her laces. "That's a big healthy baby you're carrying, Kia. Are you looking forward to seeing it?"

Kia leaned back with a sigh. "I've decided I don't want to see her. I just want you to give her to Joanna and Brett. It will be less painful that way."

The doctor nodded. "I understand where you're coming from, Kia," she said as she got up and ran the water to wash her hands. "But you know, it might be better if you did see it, and even hold it. Otherwise the birth won't seem real, and it may be harder to heal emotionally."

"I don't know. If I get her in my arms ..."

"All I'm asking is that you just think about it some more, Kia." Dr. Miyata dried her hands on some paper towel. "Saying goodbye is a good thing. It's like when someone dies we have a funeral or memorial service. It helps us accept the ending and then we can move on more easily." She paused, tossing the crumpled paper towel in the garbage. "It's certainly your choice, but spending a couple days in the hospital with the baby might ease the transition for you."

"Whatever." Kia stood, ready to leave.

"How did it go when you broke the news to the adoptive parents that you were ready to sign a contract?"

Tears sprang to Kia's eyes, and she sank back down

in the chair, but she smiled for the first time that afternoon. "It was pretty crazy." She shook her head, remembering. "Joanna and Brett couldn't stop crying, and everyone was hugging. Even Sadie the social worker got caught up in it and cried too."

"How did *you* feel?"

Kia wiped her eyes. "In a way I felt great," she said. "Like the way you feel when you give someone the perfect gift. But it's also scary because there's no turning back now. Legally I get twenty-five days after the birth to change my mind, but how could I do that to them? Yet..." Kia frowned. "I'm still scared I won't be able to hand her over. That's why I think I shouldn't even see her."

"I know you can do it."

"I wish I was so sure."

From: Kia <hazelnut@hotmail.com>
To: Justin <justintime@yahoo.com>
Date: June 16
Subject: prenatal

hi justin. prenatal is starting up again in a couple of weeks. are you still willing to be my 'partner'? i'll understand if you don't want to. my mom is really anxious to do it with me, and Joanna volunteered 2, but i'd much rather have you along. my mom's acting weird lately — way too moody! and joanna's great but i just don't want her there. i don't know why really. it's just a feeling. somehow i always feel guilty for being pregnant when she's around. feel free to analyze. :-)

i wish youth group didn't break up for the summer. i'm so bored already. shawna's gone for 2 months to camp and there's no one else i really want to be around. actually, no one wants to be around me. besides, everyone's doing sports — which I'm not into right now (duh), or working (who's gonna hire me this summer!) or partying — and i don't get invited to those anymore.

heavy sigh. yes, it's going to be a long one.
k.

From: Justin <justintime@yahoo.com>
To: Kia <hazelnut@hotmail.com>
Date: June 16
Subject: Re: prenatal

i don't need to analyze. you're doing a fine job all on your own.

yes! i'll be there for prenatal. i'd never have forgiven u if you'd replaced me. and about this summer. i could sure use some more steady volunteers at the seniors' home. interested?

From: Kia <hazelnut@hotmail.com>
To: Justin <justintime@yahoo.com>
Date: June 17
Subject: analyzing

okay, i know why i'm not invited to parties, and i guess i know why i don't want joanna at prenatal, but could you explain my mom? this is not your usual pms kind of thing. she's usually so cool but right now she just has to glance at me and she gets all choked. i can't stand it. my dad, he's another story. i'd swear he's avoiding me. i probably embarrass him, or maybe i'm just so disgusting to look at right now.

good idea about volunteering more at the seniors' home!!!

i'll stock up on the community service points. what kind of stuff can I do with them?

BFN
kia

From: Justin <justintime@yahoo.com>
To: Kia <hazelnut@hotmail.com>
Date: June 17
Subject: Re: analyzing

about your parents, ki, talk to them. they're cool, so something's up and u need to know what it is so u don't imagine the wrong stuff. go ask them. now. you'll be glad u did. what's happening with your little sister?

we'll find stuff for you to do with the seniors. not to worry.
j.

From: Kia <hazelnut@hotmail.com>
To: Justin <justintime@yahoo.com>
Date: June 17
Subject: nagging

angie's been acting weird too. she doesn't bring her friends home anymore but it doesn't take a rocket scientist to figure that one out. and you're right. i'll call a family meeting tonight. thanks for nagging. LOL.

hugs
k.

~ baby has eyebrows
~ eyelashes are developing
~ baby is regulating its own temperature
~ she's the size of a small doll

June 17

It's grief!!! It was sooo obvious but I just couldn't see it. As I get bigger and bigger the truth of what is happening is getting to all of us. I'm grieving for a lost year, lost dreams (Derek, Justin), lost friends, loss of my "body" and for (god! I don't even want to write it down!) losing her. (I wish I could erase that)

Mom & Dad are grieving for loss of control (over me), loss of their oldest "child" and loss of their first grandchild.

Angie is grieving too. She can't look up to me as the perfect sister anymore. She's ashamed. And she doesn't have me all to herself — she sees the unborn baby as some kind of competition.

So now I know what's bothering everyone, what do I do about it? Maybe I should have gone away for nine months. Maybe I should have aborted ...

No!!! I did the right thing.

Kia pushed Grace's wheelchair along the gravel path that

ran parallel to the river. When they reached the lookout point, she locked the brakes on the chair and carefully lowered herself onto a bench that overlooked the river. Only a narrow stream of water was now snaking its way past the seniors' home. The rest of the riverbed was dry and dusty.

Kia sighed and placed her hands on her large belly.

"What is it, Kia? Are you feeling okay?"

"Yeah, I'm fine." She leaned back, crossed one ankle over the other and stared out at the sluggish stream.

"How much longer before the baby arrives?"

"About five weeks."

"Probably the longest five weeks of your life." Grace leaned closer and ran her hand over Kia's tummy. "Hard to believe it can get much bigger, but it will."

"Don't remind me." Kia slouched down some more. She tilted her head back until it lay on the backrest of the bench. Her long hair almost brushed the ground as she studied the clouds. "You know, in some ways I don't even want her to be born," she said. "Right now she's all mine." She hugged her belly with both arms. "After she's born she becomes someone else's." She turned to look at Grace. "Do you have children?"

"I did. But I outlived them both. And I never even got to have grandchildren."

"Oh," Kia groaned, sitting up. "It must be awful to outlive your kids." She wiped away the tears that had sprung to her eyes.

"It is," Grace agreed. "I can't think of anything worse. I'd gladly have given my life to spare theirs."

They went back to sitting in silence, Kia studying the trickle of water and Grace studying Kia.

"What's really on your mind, Kia?" Grace said suddenly.

Kia shrugged and looked away. "I don't know. A lot of stuff, I guess." She paused, considering the question. "Grace, do you think my life will ever go back to normal?"

"What's normal?"

"The same as before."

"You'll never be the same as before, Kia," Grace said gently, "so neither will your life. Too much has happened in the last seven or eight months, and knowing you have a child out there, even if you're not raising her yourself, will change you. But that doesn't mean that your life won't be full and exciting again. It'll just be a little different."

"What about my friends? Will it ever be the same with them again?"

"With the real ones, it will."

Kia sighed. "I guess you're right."

"I know I'm right. What else is bothering you?"

"Well ..." Kia flushed and looked away. "I'm wondering if I'll ever want to be pregnant again, or if I'll even want to, you know," she looked at her feet, "have sex again."

"Aha! I bet that's what's *really* bothering you!" Grace teased.

Kia smiled shyly. "I guess it is, sort of. But ..."

"It was easier in my day," Grace interrupted. "Most of us—not all, of course—but most of us waited until we were married."

Kia tried to picture Grace as a young woman, but her joints were so gnarled and her wrinkles so deep it was impossible to conjure the image.

"But even then, Kia, it was hard. Sometimes I found myself pining to have a ... a physical relationship with someone, even when I knew it wasn't right."

Kia nodded. She understood perfectly. It was just like what she'd had with Derek.

"There was one handsome young man who didn't go overseas during the war with the others. I forget why." Kia could tell by the faraway look in Grace's eyes that she was reliving another time in her mind, but then a soft smile lit her face. "I'll never forget him. He would drop by and ask if there was anything we needed done around the house. He always seemed to know when I'd be alone…"

Kia leaned closer to Grace, whose voice had grown softer.

"But never you mind, nosey thing!" Grace said, shaking her head and bringing herself back to the present. She turned to look at Kia. "The point is, our heads are often at odds with our bodies, and it doesn't change in old age. I still feel young at heart. I'd like to jump out of this wheelchair and dance naked in the moonlight, but," she laughed at Kia's expression, "obviously I can't. When I was young and lithe, I didn't, because my head told my body not to. Now it's the other way around."

Kia smiled. "I wish you could. Then we'd see how graceful you really are."

They sat quietly for a moment, each lost in her own thoughts. "You know, Kia," Grace said, suddenly sounding serious, "I'm proud of you."

"You are?"

"Yes. You made a choice, a difficult one, but one that was right for you. And once you made your decision you could have hidden away for the duration of your pregnancy, like lots of girls do, but instead you've faced the world with your head held high. That is a brave thing to do."

Kia nodded thoughtfully. She'd never considered herself brave before. Stubborn, maybe, but not brave.

"*You* are dancing naked, Kia," Grace whispered.

"I am?" Kia asked, smiling warily.

"Yes, you are," Grace assured her. Their eyes locked, and Kia felt a strong connection. "Exposed completely. Moving to an internal rhythm, all your own."

Kia continued to look deep into Grace's eyes, trying to understand. "How did we get onto this, anyway?" she asked eventually.

"We were talking about sex."

"Actually," Kia laughed, "I think you were talking about sex."

"Whatever," Grace said. She leaned closer to Kia again. "Someday," she said, "you're going to meet just the right person. The two of you will make a commitment to each other."

"I wonder ..."

"You will. And then ..."

"Then what?"

"When you find that right person, enjoy *it*."

Kia looked puzzled. "It?"

"Your sexuality, silly girl!" Grace smiled as Kia blushed. "It's a wonderful gift," she continued, closing her eyes and sitting back in her wheelchair, "and not something to shy away from."

It was Kia's turn to study Grace. "If you could do it all again," she said, "knowing you'd outlive your kids, would you still have had them?"

"Ah yes," Grace said. "The conversation comes full

circle." She turned and looked Kia squarely in the eye. "I wouldn't have missed the experience of being a mom for anything Kia, even though ..." She stopped.

"Even though it's so hard to lose them?" Kia asked softly, looking away.

"Yes. There are different ways of losing them, I suppose. But there's no other experience like having children. Someday, honey, you should have another child. Experience parenthood. Being completely responsible for a child is something not to be missed."

Kia nodded thoughtfully.

Grace reached over and placed a twisted hand on top of Kia's. "And just think, you are giving a childless couple that same opportunity. You're not only brave, you're generous too."

Kia met Grace's eyes. "You know," she said after a moment, "you would have been an awesome grandma."

"You think so, Kia?" Grace asked, her eyes shining.

"I know so, Grace."

week 35/40

~ baby could live on the outside
~ eyes are opening and shutting
~ baby is putting on weight
~ rapid brain growth

July 23
The people at the home are so close to the end of their lives.
My baby hasn't even drawn its first breath.

Each of those old people was once someone's baby,
Wrapped in their parents' arms, loved, adored.
Wondering what life would bring them.

They were each someone's unborn baby, too
Eagerly awaited
Or?

Each of their lives were once clean slates
With endless possibilities

And now?
They sit, waiting.
Waiting for what?

Another baby will soon be born.
First breaths, last breaths
The seamlessness of life

From: Justin <justintime@yahoo.com>
To: Kia <hazelnut@hotmail.com>
Date: July 25
Subject: worried
hi ki,

when you didn't show up at the home today, everyone
got worried. beatrice thought for sure your baby had
come, and flo just kept watching the door, the book
you've been reading to her propped open in her lap.
grace was the worst. she kept twisting and twisting the
bottom of her sweater until i thought for sure she'd make
a rag out of it.

J

From: Kia <hazelnut@hotmail.com>
To: Justin <justintime@yahoo.com>
Date: July 25
Subject: Re: worried

sorry justin. i meant to tell you last night at prenatal that i
had a doctor's appointment today. i have them weekly now
because my blood pressure is a bit high and she just wants
to keep an eye on it. i meant to come by the home after my
appointment, but i felt so tired and it was so hot. i went
home and slept for a couple of hours.

you were great at prenatal. you're going to be better than
any of those 'real' dads on the big day.

K

From: Justin <justintime@yahoo.com>
To: Kia <hazelnut@hotmail.com>
Date: July 25

Subject: phew

glad you're ok. will we c u tomorrow?

J

From: Kia <hazelnut@hotmail.com>
To: Justin <justintime@yahoo.com>
Date: July 25
Subject: Re: phew

trust me. i'll b there!

k

week 36/40

~ baby gets hiccups
~ lungs are mature
~ gums are becoming rigid
~ fat is dimpling on elbows and knees

July 28
*I'm scared. It's going to hurt so much! The birth, the
adoption, everything!*
I don't want to be me.

From: Kia <hazelnut@hotmail.com>
To: Justin <justintime@yahoo.com>
Date: Aug. 4
Subject: venting

hi justin, don't read any further if you're expecting a cheerful
letter. i need to vent. i'm sorry it's always u i dump on.

i just got back from joanna and brett's. they have an
awesome home and u should see the nursery they've put
together. it looks like something out of a magazine. i kept
imagining my little baby lying in the cradle they have, with
the winnie-the-pooh mobile hanging over it and all the little
stuffed animals sitting in the end. i could smell the ivory
snow soap that joanna used to wash everything. she's even
got the little sleeper laid out that she's bringing her home
in. it's yellow. yellow is good for a girl or a boy, she said. i

guess she doesn't believe it's going to be a girl.

i made the mistake of sitting in the rocking chair and pretending that it would be me rocking my baby to sleep. i actually felt sick i was so jealous, and it's confusing, because i really like them. but i hate them too! that should be my nursery! this is my baby but they've gone ahead and got everything ready, like it was already theirs.

and then i heard them arguing in the kitchen! i couldn't believe it. they obviously didn't know i could hear them — they thought i was still in the nursery. maybe they're not so perfect after all. maybe i shouldn't trust them with my baby!!!

o justin. i know how stupid i sound. my split personality is at it again. half of me knows how lucky i am to have found them, the other half is still telling me not to let her go. there. i'm done. thanks for listening. what would I do without you?

k.

From: Justin <justintime@yahoo.com>
To: Kia <hazelnut@hotmail.com>
Date: Aug. 4
Subject: Re: venting

your feelings are ok, ki, completely normal and it's a good thing that you're venting. i'm always here 2 listen. Speaking of venting, have you been practicing your breathing? i want us to b the best. don't let me down!

J.

From: Kia <hazelnut@hotmail.com>
To: Justin <justintime@yahoo.com>

Date: Aug. 4
Subject: breathing
i'll be the best breather there. trust me.

k

⌒

Kia closed *Charlotte's Web* and sighed. She glanced at the faces of the seniors gathered around her. She understood now why Justin had chosen this particular book. She didn't miss the parallel between Charlotte, the spider, entrusting her sac of eggs to Wilbur, the pig, with her own situation, but she thought the story of Charlotte getting old and dying might be depressing for some of these seniors. And why a children's book?

"That was beautiful, Kia," Flo said, wiping her eyes. "It is quite a different story when you hear it in old age."

"Uh-huh," agreed Grace. "E.B. White has such a magical way with words. He describes the passage of time so beautifully."

"I know what you mean," Beatrice said. "Can you find that paragraph again, Kia, the one about how you feel when you're waiting for something to happen?"

Kia flipped through the last couple of pages until she spotted it. She read, "*For Wilbur, nothing in life was so important as this small round object—nothing else mattered. Patiently he awaited the end of winter and the coming of the little spiders. Life is always a rich and steady time when you are waiting for something to happen or to hatch.*"

Kia looked up and met Grace's eyes. Grace smiled and nodded. Kia had to look away as a wave of guilt washed over her. Joanna was like Wilbur, waiting for the baby to be born, but she, Kia, kept pushing her away.

"And now read the last paragraph again, Kia," Grace said quietly.

"*Wilbur never forgot Charlotte,*" Kia read. "*Although he loved her children and grandchildren dearly, none of the new spiders ever quite took her place in his heart. She was in a class by herself. It is not often that someone comes along who is a true friend and a good writer. Charlotte was both.*" Kia closed the book.

"True friends are rare," Justin commented as he joined the small group.

Kia nodded. "That's for sure."

"Although I think there is a Charlotte or two in everyone's life," he added.

Kia nodded, knowing full well that no one would ever take Justin's place in her heart. He was definitely in a class by himself.

〜

Kia lay on her side on the thin mat. Justin knelt beside her. Around the room panting could be heard from the pregnant women as they practiced the breathing techniques that would get them through labor.

"Why do you think no one visits our seniors, Justin? It's so pathetic."

"*Our* seniors?" Justin smiled down at her.

"Yeah. *Our* seniors. What makes them all yours?"

He laughed. "Nothing. It's great that you've adopted them." He stopped abruptly, realizing, from Kia's sharp glance, that it was a poor choice of words, but then continued, "You know what I mean, and most of them do get occasional visitors. It doesn't seem like much, I know, but everyone leads busy lives. I think most families do their best. And I don't think they'd want you feeling sorry for them. Just enjoy their company."

Kia nodded. "I've enjoyed spending more time there." She smiled, thinking of Grace. "I think I'm getting more out of it than the seniors. Now I'd do it even if I wasn't earning community service points."

"Funny how that happens," Justin replied. "Now lie down and get back to work."

Kia sat up instead. She reached out and gently punched his arm. "How'd you get so smart anyhow?"

He punched her back. "Just born that way, I guess," he said. "You got the looks, I got the brains. Don't we make a great team?"

Kia laughed, looking down at herself. "Oh yeah. I'm, like, real gorgeous. And are you saying I don't have a brain?"

Justin shook his head, smiling. "No. I saw your last report card, remember? I wish I'd done half so well in school."

"It's weird, isn't it? I know people who get great marks, but I wouldn't call them smart. Know what I mean?"

"I know exactly."

Kia rubbed her stomach. "I hope my little girl gets the kind of smarts you have."

"And your looks," Justin said. "Although," he added with a laugh, "she won't be doing half bad if she looks like her dad."

"Don't remind me of Derek," Kia said, easing herself

back onto her mat as she spotted the teacher approaching them. "I hope she's nothing like him."

"She is half him, Ki," Justin reminded her quietly, as he leaned over her. "And have you talked to him about signing the adoption papers yet? Time's running out."

"No," she said with a sigh. "But I will. When I get a chance."

~

But Kia's chance never came.

Dr. Miyata frowned when she read the dial on the blood-pressure monitor during Kia's weekly appointment.

"What's the matter?"

"Your blood pressure isn't good. You've got a condition known as pre-eclampsia." The doctor squeezed one of Kia's ankles. The indentations took a moment too long to return to normal. "Your swollen ankles are another symptom of it."

"Pre-eclampsia? What does that mean?"

"It's a complication that can occur in pregnancy and can lead to convulsions and even coma. It is often characterized by high blood pressure. Usually we can treat it with just rest." The doctor stepped away from the examining table and sat on the stool. She stared at Kia's file for a moment. "I think we need to get you a specialist. An obstetrician."

"Does that mean you won't be delivering my baby?"

"No, I'll be there. I'll assist. But your health, not the baby, is my concern right now. I'm going to admit you into the hospital immediately, and the specialist can see you there."

"The hospital? I've got to go to the hospital already?"

"It's just a precaution, Kia. Bed rest might be all it takes to keep your blood pressure at a safe level. But at the rate it's rising, I think it needs constant monitoring."

"Oh." Kia felt numb. It had never occurred to her that her pregnancy wouldn't progress exactly as they described it in prenatal classes. Going to the hospital before labor started was not the proper order.

"There's something I'd like to do first."

"I'll give you three hours," the doctor said. "And then I'll expect you to be at the hospital. I'll try to get an obstetrician to see you there this afternoon."

Kia's mind was whirling as she left the examining room. It would take her a good hour just to get home on the bus. She thought of calling Justin—he'd come for sure—but she didn't want to take him away from the seniors. She paged her mom at her university class instead.

As Kia stared out the window of the clinic she saw Mrs. Hazelwood squeal into the Superstore parking lot. She glanced at her watch. It had only taken her half an hour from classroom to clinic, an amazing feat considering the distance and usual traffic congestion. Her mom pulled the car up to the front of the clinic, a no-parking zone, wheels straddling the sidewalk. She left the engine running as she hopped out and ran around to open the passenger door for Kia.

"I'm just going to run in and talk to the doctor myself," she said as Kia came out of the clinic and climbed into the car. "I want to find out exactly what's going on."

"Never mind, Mom. The doctor said it's not that serious. They just want to monitor me." Kia hated the trace of irritation she heard in her own voice, but she couldn't help it. Why was it that she had to calm her mom down, instead of the other way around? "Let's go. We can talk in the car."

Mrs. Hazelwood hesitated, studied Kia's determined face and reluctantly slid back into the driver's seat.

"Can you stop at the seniors' home, Mom? I want to tell everyone what's happening."

"I think we should go straight to the hospital, Ki. Justin can pass messages on for you."

"No," she said, crossing her arms. "I want to see them myself."

Her mom sighed, but took the turn-off that led to the Willows Intermediate Care Home. "You've got exactly five minutes," she said, parking the car in a handicapped stall. She was about to leap out to assist her daughter, but Kia grabbed her arm and pulled her back.

"I can do it myself." With as much dignity as she could muster, Kia struggled out of the car. She saw her mom reach for the cell phone and snapped. "Who are you calling?"

"I'm just going to have your dad meet us at the hospital. I'll call the Reverend and Sadie too."

"Don't even think of it, Mom," Kia said, slamming the door and leaning in the open window. "I'm not having the baby yet. And I'm not dying, either. I told you—my blood pressure is being monitored, that's all. Relax. Don't call anyone." But when she glanced over her shoulder as she pulled open the door to the seniors' home, she could see her mom already talking to someone on the phone. Her reaction was making Kia wonder if her mom knew something about pre-eclampsia that she didn't. A chill ran down her spine and she shuddered, even in the August heat.

Kia made her way, stomach first, across the sunroom toward the group of seniors. Justin was sitting with them.

"You're here early," he said, glancing at his watch. "Everything go okay at the doctor's?"

"That's why I'm here," she said. She looked around at the old faces she'd come to care so much about. "My blood pressure is getting a little too high and I have to go into the hospital to have it monitored. I may be in there until after the baby is born, so I wanted to come in to say goodbye, for now."

They all stared at her quietly for a moment. Kia wondered if it was concern that she saw flicker across a few of the faces. Flo was the first to find her voice. "All the best, Kia," she said in her wobbly voice. "We'll be thinking of you. I hope she's a healthy little girl."

"Yes," said Bert, looking around at the group. "We'll all miss you, so you get back here pronto, okay? We'll have some kind of party, right Justin?"

"You know me, a regular party animal," Justin agreed, winking at Bert.

Kia went around to each member of the group, hugging her friends and accepting their warm words of encouragement. When she got to Grace she straightened the blanket that lay across her knees and ran her fingers down one wrinkled cheek. Grace opened her mouth to speak, but a wracking cough overcame her. Kia waited patiently beside the wheelchair. She pulled a tissue out of the package that the old woman kept tucked beside her and wiped the drool from the side of her wizened mouth.

"You go, girl," Grace said quietly when she was able to talk again.

"I will," Kia said, smiling at her choice of words. Grace reached out and stroked Kia's huge belly. "You're a lovely young lady. Everything's going to be fine."

"I know." Tears pricked at the back of Kia's eyes. With a quick wave, she turned and walked back the way she'd come, with Justin at her side.

"Is Grace okay?" she asked him.

"I don't know." He frowned. "We've got a doctor coming to look at her today. I don't like the sound of that cough."

"You let me know what's going on."

"I will. And how about you? Are you okay?"

"Yeah, but my mom's getting to me. She's all freaked out."

"You're her little girl. She loves you. Moms all freak when they're worried about their babies."

Kia rolled her eyes and stepped aside as Justin opened the door for her. He greeted her mom, and helped Kia into the car. "I'll come by the hospital tonight," he said into the open car window. "Don't go having the baby without me. I'm your labor coach, remember?"

"Trust me. I'm not doing it without you," she said. "When the time comes, I'll keep my legs tightly crossed until you get there."

week 38/40

~ wrinkles are disappearing from the baby's face
~ average-sized baby will weigh about six pounds
and be fourteen inches long

Aug. 14
She called me courageous and generous. What a joke. I'm
scared and greedy. I don't want to share my baby. I want
her all to myself.

"Anywhere between thirty-eight and forty-two weeks is considered full term," the doctor explained, "and you're at thirty-eight weeks. The baby is large and seems healthy. It's your health that's compromised now."

Kia nodded. She'd been in the hospital for three days, but things had only gotten worse. Her ankles were so swollen that her legs reminded her of a hippo's, and her blood pressure had increased steadily.

"So tomorrow's the day," Dr. McBride, the obstetrician, said. "Your baby's birthday will likely be August fifteenth."

Kia nodded. "She'll be a Leo. Cool." She was relieved to be getting it over with.

"Good. Tomorrow then, first thing, we'll hook you up to an IV and start the drip. The drug we use is called Pitocin. It's a natural hormone that induces labor. I'm afraid you'll have to stay in bed because you'll be wired to an electronic fetal-monitoring machine. We have to keep a close eye on the baby." He studied her face. "Any questions?"

"Will Justin be able to stay with me through the whole thing?"

"Yes, unless there's an emergency which requires us to do a Caesarian section, but I'm not anticipating that."

"Me neither."

"And I understand," he said quietly, "that you're putting the baby up for adoption."

She looked away.

"Do you want to see it?"

Kia paused before she answered. "I wasn't going to, but …"

"I think you should," he said. "It's healing to say goodbye."

Kia didn't answer.

"How about the adopting parents? Do you want them at the delivery?"

"No. She's going to be theirs soon enough."

"That's fair. The fewer people present, the better it is for me. But I like to check, just to be certain. I'm sure they're going to be anxious."

Kia nodded. "My parents will be anxious too."

"And a social worker?" he asked. "I suppose you have one of those?"

"Uh-huh." Kia smiled, just a little. "But I don't think Sadie will be anxious. In fact, she might be just the person to keep everyone else calm."

"Then let's make sure she's here," the doctor said, smiling.

"Oh, and then there's the Rev, and my little sister."

"That is what waiting rooms are for."

Kia nodded.

"Everything's going to be just fine, Kia," Dr. McBride said one more time. "You'll go back to school in the fall a little older and a little wiser."

"And a little lighter, I hope," Kia said.

"That's a given," he said. "I'll see you in the morning. Try to have a good rest tonight. Tomorrow could be a long day."

Joanna and Brett spent the evening with Kia in her hospital room, discussing baby names. They were determined to find one they all liked. Justin sat crossed-legged on the floor in a corner, quietly listening to the discussion. Kia's parents had gone home awhile earlier, with promises to be at the hospital early the following morning.

"Why don't you choose a couple boys' names, just in case?" Joanna suggested.

Kia shook her head. "I don't need to."

"Then tell me what names on my list you like."

"They're all fine," Kia said, hardly glancing at the page that was placed in front of her.

"You know," Justin said, adding his opinion for the first time all evening, "I've heard people say that it's better to see the baby before you choose the name. Some names just don't suit some babies."

Joanna sighed. "I guess you're right, Justin. We do have a list of ten names we've all agreed on. Maybe one of them will jump out when we see it."

"When we see *her*," Kia corrected.

Brett shook his head. "I've never known anyone so sure of an unborn baby's gender. What makes you so certain, Ki?"

"I've known from the start," she answered. "But it's not something I can explain."

"We'll forgive you if you're wrong, you know," Brett said, smiling. "But how will you feel if it's a boy?"

"It's not going to be a boy," Kia answered, perfectly serious.

"Kia's never wrong about anything," Justin teased. "She gets it from her father."

Kia stuck her tongue out at him. "You're just jealous."

Joanna closed the baby-name book she was thumbing through. She came over, sat on the bed beside Kia and picked up her hand.

"How are you feeling about tomorrow, honey?" she asked.

Kia tugged her hand away. She shrugged.

Joanna persisted. "I think we should talk about it."

"Okay, then. If you really want to know the truth, I'm scared stiff," Kia answered crossly, facing Joanna. "And sad."

"Sad?"

"Yeah, once she's born you're going to take her away." Kia glanced at Justin and then back at Joanna. "Right now she's all mine." She rubbed her huge stomach.

Joanna nodded and got up off the bed. She went over to stand beside Brett.

"You're giving her to us to raise, Kia," Brett said, "but we're not taking her away. You know you'll always be welcome in our home. You can spend as much time with her as you want."

Kia lay back on the bed. "I know, but it's just not the same."

Reverend Petrenko knocked and entered the room. "Hello everyone," he said, looking around. "Did I interrupt something?" he asked, sensing the somber mood of the small group.

"We're discussing tomorrow, and what happens after the baby is born," Brett answered after shaking the Reverend's hand. "Kia just shared her feelings with us. She says she's scared and sad."

"And I really don't feel like *sharing* anything else tonight," Kia said, unable to disguise her irritation. "I think I need to go to sleep now."

"I'll just stay a minute," the Reverend said. "And I won't ask you to share anything, Kia," he teased gently. "I just wanted to know how you all felt about having a small ceremony to mark the occasion of the adoption."

Kia frowned. "Huh?"

"I have a small service prepared. We could use the hospital chapel, and just the three or four of you," he glanced at Justin, "would attend, with the new baby."

"What would we have to do?" Kia asked.

"Not much," the Reverend answered. "At one point in the service I would ask you if you have anything you wish to say to your new baby or to Joanna and Brett. I'd then ask them the same thing. The rest would be me trying to mark this occasion as a sacred event in all your lives."

Brett and Joanna glanced at each other. "I think it's a beautiful idea," Brett said. "How about you, Kia?"

She rolled onto her side, her back to Joanna and Brett and her arms wrapped around her belly. She lifted one arm just long enough to wipe her nose with the back of her hand. "Whatever."

Justin got up and began to rub her back. "We'll be there," he told the Reverend. "All three of us. And with Joanna and Brett, that makes five."

⌒

Kia heaved herself off the hospital bed and shuffled to the bathroom. When she came out she put on her new bathrobe, a gift from Joanna and Brett. She sat in the chair in the corner of the room. She knew it must be close to midnight. The hospital was fairly quiet, although she could hear the low murmur of the nurses' voices in their station and the odd beep of a call button. Occasionally a wailing baby was wheeled past her room in its hospital bassinet. She wished she could sleep—it would pass the time more quickly—but sleep eluded her tonight.

Eventually she got up, took a quarter out of the drawer in the night table and padded down the hallway to the pay phone. She dropped the quarter in the slot and dialed the number.

"Hello?" Her mother answered after one ring, her voice anxious.

"Hi, Mom. It's me."

"Kia! Is everything okay?"

"Yeah. I just couldn't sleep. I'm sorry I'm calling so late. Did I wake you up?"

"No, no. Dad and I can't sleep either. We're sitting in the kitchen drinking tea."

Kia pictured them in the cozy kitchen, sitting across the table from each other, the back door open to let in the cool night breeze. Suddenly she felt her eyes brimming with tears. "I wish I was there with you," she said, not trying to mask the quiver in her voice. She felt like a little kid, but she didn't care. "I feel so lonely here."

"Oh, Kia. We'll come right over." Her mom's voice quivered too.

"No, no, Mom!" Kia quickly recovered. "I'm okay, really. Just wanted to call and tell you how much ... how much I love you. And Dad."

"We know that, honey. And we love you too. You know that, right?"

"Yeah. And I'm sorry for everything I've put you through."

"Kia, are you sure everything is okay?"

"Uh-huh. Really."

"We'll be there first thing in the morning."

"I know."

"It's going to be okay."

"How do you know that?" The quiver was back in her voice, and it occurred to her that she was more nervous about the birth than she'd realized.

"I just do. You have the best doctor, you're in the hospital, and you're a healthy, strong girl." She paused. "Are you sure you don't want me to come over and stay with you tonight?"

"No, Mom. We both better get some sleep. Give Dad a hug for me. I'll see you in a couple of hours."

"Okay, Kia. Love you."

Kia hung up and drew in a ragged breath. It was

going to be a long night.

The nursery was just down the hall, and she went and stood at the viewing window. There weren't many babies there—most of them were in their mothers' rooms—but the few that remained were sleeping soundly. A nurse was moving from one bassinet to the next, checking on them. She spotted Kia and nodded at the door. Kia went to the locked door and waited for it to open.

"Are you having trouble sleeping?" the nurse asked. "Would you like to come in?"

Kia nodded and stepped into the room. It was warm and bright, and the sweet smell of newborns filled the room.

"Yours hasn't come yet," the nurse observed. "Are you having a C-section?"

"No, I'm being induced tomorrow," Kia answered, moving farther into the nursery. She stood beside a bassinet, looking down at the tiny dark-skinned baby.

"So by tomorrow night yours might be in here too. Or maybe you'll want to keep it in your room, though I always think the new moms should get a good night's sleep before they go home, but I'm old-fashioned in my thinking," she murmured. "Nowadays the new moms are packed up and shipped out before they even have a chance to catch their breath," she added.

"Mine won't be coming home with me," Kia said, moving to another bassinet. The baby in it started to squirm.

The nurse glanced at the chart hanging on the side of the bassinet and then at the clock on the wall. "He's due for a bottle feed," the nurse said. "Do you want to do it?"

Kia watched the baby as it woke up. Its cries were

raw and insistent. "Sure," she said, anxious to make him stop crying.

"Then scrub your hands, put on a mask and go sit in that rocking chair," the nurse instructed. "I'll get his formula ready."

Kia did as she was told. A moment later the nurse handed her the little bundle and a small glass bottle with a nipple attached. "You'll have to hold him up high," she said, smiling as Kia tried to position the baby. "Above your stomach. Or off to the side, perhaps."

Kia found a comfortable position and put the nipple to the frantic baby's mouth. She watched as he latched on and began to suck hungrily. Her surrogate baby—the bag of dog food—hadn't felt anything like this. This baby was warm as he nuzzled into her. He regarded her with his wide, wise-looking eyes. She sensed he knew she wasn't his mom, but he didn't mind her feeding him. She leaned over and pressed her cheek to his forehead. Even through the mask he smelled wonderful, but she realized, with a start, that she didn't feel a bond with him. He was someone else's baby, not hers. He was pleasant to hold, but it was not as she imagined it would be with her own. She wondered if this was how Joanna would feel when she fed Kia's baby. Would her baby know that Joanna wasn't her real mom? Would she feel abandoned right from day one?

Kia began to rock in the chair as she fed the tiny newborn. She watched as the nurse prepared a bottle for a second baby and then joined her in another rocking chair.

"You've got a great job," Kia said, talking through the mask. "Taking care of all these babies."

The nurse smiled as she pushed the rubber nipple

into the baby's mouth. "Yeah, on quiet nights, like this one, it's the best job in the world."

"So it's not always like this?"

"No. This is a rare quiet night. Sometimes two or three new ones arrive all at once, and they all need attention immediately. That usually happens when it's feeding time for the ones already in here. They all start squawking at once. I can call the nurses' station for help, but it's never enough. You just have to deal with one baby at a time and hope that no emergencies arise."

Kia nodded, watching as the baby she held closed its eyes but didn't stop sucking.

"So your baby is being adopted?" the nurse asked.

"Yeah. I guess."

"You guess?"

Kia shrugged. "Yeah, it is. I just keep hoping for a miracle."

The nurse cocked her head. "A miracle?"

"I've been trying for almost nine months to figure out how I can keep her and raise her myself."

"Not an easy thing to do. How old are you?"

"Seventeen."

"You're not much older than that little guy you're holding."

"Very funny." Kia gave the nurse her nastiest look, then smiled. They continued to rock and feed the babies in comfortable silence.

"Is it an open adoption? Do you know who the parents will be?"

"Yeah. They're great. I chose them myself." Kia laughed. "And now I hate their guts."

The nurse shot Kia a curious look.

"They're too good. They're everything I'm not."

"Too good? Is that possible when you're choosing parents for your baby?"

"No." Kia pulled the nipple out of the baby's mouth. He was fast asleep again. She held him up to her shoulder and patted his back. "I just wish I could trade places with them."

"You look like you know what you're doing."

"I've been practicing with a bag of dog food." Kia glanced at the nurse's expression and then had to laugh. The baby began to fuss, so she cradled him and popped the nipple back into his mouth. "It's a long story," she explained. "The real thing is a lot nicer."

"I guess so," the nurse said, beginning to rock her chair again. "A bag of dog food. What will they think of next?"

⟡

Kia settled the baby back in its bassinet and left the nursery. She went into her dark room and jumped, startled, when a figure, sitting in the chair, stood up.

"Justin! What are you doing here?"

"Shh," he said. "I was in the neighborhood, so I thought I'd drop by. The nurses think I'm the baby's father so they didn't throw me out."

"But it's the middle of the night! You should be home sleeping. I'm going to need you wide awake tomorrow."

"Good point, Kia. So why aren't you in bed? You gave me quite the scare when I didn't find you here. Then I had a look around and saw you through the window in the nursery."

"I couldn't sleep. I can't get comfortable. You should try lying on this stupid mattress with a water-filled beach ball sticking out of you."

"No thanks. But you should at least be resting."

"Okay. I'm lying down." Kia tossed her housecoat onto the foot of the bed, climbed in and lay on her side. She patted the spot beside her for Justin to sit on. "So why are you here? Worried about me?"

"No. You're going to be just fine."

"Oh yeah?"

"Yeah." Justin paused, then continued quietly. "But Grace isn't."

Kia was sure her heart stopped for a moment. "Grace? What is it?"

"She's been moved up to Palliative Care from the ER." He sighed, and Kia could see the tears in his eyes. "I was just up there. She hasn't got long."

"But I saw her just a few days ago! When I stopped off to say goodbye."

"The cancer's all through her now. It's just a matter of time."

"Cancer?"

"Uh-huh. She's had it awhile, but her health is too fragile to handle any treatment so she's just letting nature take its course."

"I didn't know …"

"No, she didn't talk about it."

Kia thought about Grace's wracking cough and remembered how tired she'd looked.

"I'm sorry." Justin ran his hand over Kia's tummy. "I shouldn't have dumped that news on you tonight …"

"Oh! You're back." A nurse burst into the room, clutching a blood-pressure gauge. "I thought maybe you'd changed your mind about having a baby."

Kia tried to smile as the nurse wrapped the band around her arm, but it was too hard to force it. She watched as the nurse jotted something on her chart. "Well?"

"It's dropped, just a little. That's a good thing."

Kia nodded.

"You should try to get some sleep." She glanced sharply at Justin.

He cleared his throat. "I know," he said. "Just checking up on her." He stood up. "I'll see you bright and early, Ki."

She nodded. The lump in her throat was too big to swallow.

He leaned over the bed and kissed her forehead. "Go to sleep. You need to look fabulous for your baby when she sees you for the first time."

Kia gave Justin a little shove. With one last look over his shoulder, he left the room.

Kia lay in stunned silence. Grace, *her* Grace, was lying two floors above her, waiting to die. What did that feel like? Was she scared? And how ironic that she was down here, on the verge of giving birth to a new life as Grace was coming to the end of hers.

Kia wiped away the tear that meandered down her cheek. She turned on the reading light and reached for the journal that sat on the table beside her bed. Propping herself up on her elbow, she again ran her fingers over the notebook's grainy cover. She opened it to the first page and read the entry. Then she read the next entry, and the next. With sudden clarity, she realized that her journal was like a detailed roadmap of the emotional detour she'd taken in the past eight months. The gamut of her emotions was described in these pages, from the horror of discovering she was pregnant to the elation she'd experienced when she first felt the baby move inside her. It also showed her increasing love for the unborn baby, as well as her struggle as she faced giving it up for adoption. Kia knew what she had to do. Opening to the next blank page, she picked up her pen and began to write one final entry. When she was done, she gently closed the journal, put it away and turned out the light.

She lay back on her pillow, but was acutely aware of how light her room still was. Glancing at the window, she started when she saw that the moon was now directly in her line of vision. Almost full, it hung in the night sky. She wondered if Grace was seeing it too.

Kia climbed out of bed and pulled on her housecoat. She left her room and headed down the hall, but in the opposite direction of the nursery. When she got to the bank of elevators she pushed the button on the wall.

Reaching the sixth floor, she quietly slipped past the nurses' station and began to peek into each room. It didn't take long to find Grace. She was lying in bed, her eyes were closed, and a nurse was standing beside her, taking her pulse. The nurse looked up, startled at seeing Kia in the doorway.

"Are you lost, dear?" she asked quietly.

"Kia!" Grace said, her lids blinking open before Kia could answer the nurse. Kia caught a glimpse of Grace's glassy eyes before a horrible coughing and hacking overwhelmed the frail body. Her eyes shut again as she struggled to breathe. Kia was shocked to see how much sicker she'd become in just a few days.

The nurse waited patiently for Grace to recover before she spoke to Kia again. "Where are you supposed to be?" she asked.

"The maternity ward, but I heard Grace was here and I wanted to see her."

"It's getting awfully late," the nurse said, glancing at her watch.

"I'll only stay five minutes," Kia promised.

"I'll kick her out if she stays a second longer," Grace promised the nurse, while smiling at Kia.

"Okay. Five minutes. That's it."

Kia pulled a chair up to Grace's bed as soon as the nurse left.

"Oh, Grace. Justin told me you were here."

"I'm glad you came up, Kia. I wanted to see you."

Kia reached out and picked up the old woman's hand. "Are you in pain, Grace?"

She shook her head. "No, not at all. Whatever medication I'm on is working beautifully."

Kia realized then that it was the medication that was making Grace's old eyes shine so unnaturally.

"I wanted you to know how special you are to me, Kia," Grace said, her voice soft.

"You're special to me too, Grace."

"I hope you don't mind, but I've secretly thought of you as the grandchild I never had," she said. "And your baby is like my great-grandchild."

Kia squeezed Grace's hand, but her shoulders slumped. "Another child taken away from you."

"No, Kia. This one will be out there, living, breathing. It's wonderful to know that."

Kia nodded. "I'm going to bring her up to see you."

Grace nodded, her eyelids beginning to droop. "That would be wonderful, Kia. I do want to see her." Then her eyes closed completely and Kia felt her hand go limp. She leaned over and kissed the sleeping woman's forehead, then quietly left the room.

⤳

Weeks later, when Kia would look back on the morning of August fifteenth, only a blur of images would come to mind, like the faces of the people who came and went: her mom and dad, Joanna and Brett and the changing parade of nurses monitoring her progress. She'd see herself as if from a distance—a disconnected, almost out-of-body experience—lying on the bed, comfortable at first, but feeling growing discomfort as the contractions increased, and then, mostly naked and slippery with sweat, crying and swearing at Justin.

At the height of the pain, her memory of the day would become even more hazy, although she would vaguely recall being wheeled to the delivery room and seeing Dr. Miyata and Dr. McBride there. Her legs were spread apart under the bright lights. She'd remember bearing down, straining until she felt she'd burst, then being told to take a huge breath and to push again. Finally, after what would seem like forever, the last horrendous push came, and the feeling of the baby sliding out. "It's a girl," someone had said, laying it on her stomach. She and Justin had laughed and cried and said they already knew that.

That is where the jumbled collection of memories ended. Everything from that moment on and for the next few days became, for Kia, crystal clear, every detail etched in her memory for life.

～

The surge of love she felt for the tiny, wrinkled baby in her arms was staggering. It had been checked over, cleaned and wrapped tightly. Now she stared into the baby's face, dumbstruck by the overwhelming power of the moment. This was the baby that her body had created and nurtured since it was just a mass of cells. This was the baby that she'd visualized and talked to, that had completely occupied her mind for so many months. Kia pulled back the infant's knitted white cap. A mass of wet black hair was stuck to her head. She loosened the towel and drew out an arm. The tiny, clenched fist immediately found its way to her mouth, and the thumb popped right in.

Kia looked up at Justin. "Just like in the picture," she said.

Justin, she could see now, was struggling to maintain his composure. He'd been strong for her all day, but now he looked like he was going to crumple, about to give in to his fatigue.

"Sit down, Justin," she said, making room on the cot beside her. He obeyed willingly.

"Do you want to hold her?" she asked.

He nodded and took the baby from her. "She's perfect," he said, his voice husky. "She looks just like you."

Kia peered at the tiny face in Justin's arms. Suddenly, the eyes blinked open and stared back at her.

"They're blue," she said, amazed.

"They sure are," said Dr. Miyata, who'd joined them and stood quietly admiring the baby. "Although they can change over the next few months."

But Kia knew they wouldn't. Those were Derek's eyes—not quite as blue, perhaps, but his eyes nonetheless.

A little later, Brett and Joanna knocked on the door and stepped into her room. The baby was sleeping in a bassinet beside the bed, and Kia's parents excused themselves and went to find coffee. Justin had gone home shortly after the birth. Kia watched as Joanna and Brett approached the bassinet.

"Oh, Kia," Joanna said, her eyes welling with tears, "she's beautiful."

Kia nodded. She watched Brett's reaction. He regarded the baby quietly and then turned to her. "Well done, kiddo."

Kia smiled back. Somehow she felt less jealous of Brett.

"Go ahead," Kia said to Joanna. "Pick her up."

Joanna's face took on the awestruck look of a small child at Christmas. She paused, smiled nervously at Kia, then gently lifted the tiny baby out of her bed. She held her close, breathing in the sweet new-baby smells. Kia watched her closely, wondering if Joanna would feel the same ambivalence toward this baby as Kia had with the little guy she'd fed late last night. But Joanna's reaction was entirely different. The tears she'd managed to hold back a moment ago could no longer be contained. They spilled down her face as she turned to her husband. "Oh,

Brett, look at her. She's so perfect."

Kia watched as Brett reached out to take her from Joanna. He swallowed hard. The two of them reminded Kia of herself and Justin that afternoon. There was no doubt that they'd already made a connection with this tiny person.

"She's got blue eyes," Kia said.

"No kidding," Brett said. "Isn't that strange?"

"Her dad's eyes are blue, and so are my dad's. I guess that makes it possible."

"I guess so." Brett passed the baby back to his wife. She sat on the edge of Kia's bed. "Have you thought anymore about the names, Kia?"

She nodded. "Justin pointed out that one of the names on our list, Brenna, means raven. And look at her hair. It couldn't get more raven-like than that."

Joanna nodded, stroking the mass of silky black hair.

"Do you still like that name?" Kia asked.

Joanna looked at Brett and he nodded. "We love it, Kia," she said. "And we were thinking that we'd like her middle name to be Kia."

Kia smiled sadly. "Thanks. I appreciate that. I really do. But I was hoping her middle name could be Grace."

Joanna and Brett looked at each other and then back at Kia.

"After a very special friend," Kia explained.

"Brenna Grace. I like the sound of it," Brett said.

Joanna nodded. "I do too. Brenna Grace it is then," she said. She looked at the new baby and whispered, "Welcome to the world, Brenna."

～

Although the nursery was too far down the hall for Kia to actually hear the babies, she woke up late that evening with an urgent need to go and check on Brenna. Tapping lightly on the nursery window, she got the attention of the nurse, the same one who'd been on duty the night before. She opened the door for Kia and smiled.

"Look at you!" she said. "You've had your baby."

Kia nodded, but her eyes were scanning the bassinets, looking for Brenna. It seemed like all the babies were awake and crying, and the sound of them made Kia anxious. Her breasts felt heavy and her nipples ached. She spotted Brenna's mop of hair and hurried over to her. Sure enough, she was wailing and wiggling around in her small bed. Her head was jammed up into a corner. Kia leaned over the baby and spoke, "Shh, Brenna, it's okay. I'm here." She watched in amazement as Brenna abruptly stopped crying, as if listening to her voice. Kia reached in and picked her up. Cradling her in her arms, she continued talking. "Everything's going to be okay. I'm here now." The baby stared up at Kia, wide-eyed. Kia continued to talk, delighted that the baby responded to her voice. "Are you hungry? Is it time for your bottle?"

"Do you want to feed her?" the nurse asked. "And change her diaper?" She'd come up beside Kia, carrying another baby. "I could use the help tonight."

"Yeah, sure," Kia answered. Putting the baby down, she unwrapped her and pulled up the tiny hospital gown. Her skin was a beautiful tan color, just as she had imagined. She counted the fingers and toes again. She changed the diaper and then studied the remains of the umbilical cord that was once attached to her own body. Then she dressed her and wrapped her up tightly.

"You won't need the mask, not for your own baby," the nurse said. "But it's always a good idea to wash your hands first. The formula and bottles are over on the counter. You can get yourself started."

Kia lay Brenna back down while she washed her hands and fixed the bottle. She had resumed crying by the time Kia got back to her, but, once again, just the sound of Kia's voice was enough to make her stop.

This time it was much easier to make herself comfortable in the rocking chair, with a smaller, softer stomach to contend with. Kia pushed the nipple into her baby's mouth and began to rock the chair. She felt complete. She hoped Brenna would take forever to drink the formula.

The nurse came over with another baby and they sat together again, just as they had the night before.

"How did it go today?" she asked Kia.

"It was hell. I'll never do it again," Kia answered.

"New moms always say that right after the birth, but it doesn't take long to forget the pain. Mostly what you'll remember is the miracle of having had a baby."

Kia didn't answer. In a day or two she wouldn't have a baby any longer. She'd be left with only the bittersweet memories of the birth.

"Are you sore?" the nurse asked gently.

Kia nodded. "Oh, yeah." Sore was putting it mildly.

"And have you started the pills to dry up your milk? Sometimes they make you feel a bit nauseous."

"I took some," she answered, "but when I came in

here I think I felt like ... like I had milk anyway."

"That's normal. It will take a few days for your body to figure out that it's not required to make it."

Kia nodded again. She and Brenna were looking right into each other's eyes. She wished she could hold onto this moment forever. A few seconds later, though, the baby's eyelids closed and Kia pulled the nipple out of her mouth, propped her on her shoulder and gently patted her back. Then she cradled her again and returned the nipple to her mouth. The baby sucked, but didn't wake up.

"I'd swear she recognized my voice when I talked to her," Kia said.

"It wouldn't surprise me," the nurse answered. "She's been listening to you talk for months."

They rocked in silence, even after Brenna had finished her bottle. Kia didn't want to return to her lonely room.

Glancing out the window she noticed the huge moon again. It made her remember Grace, two floors up. That gave her an idea.

"I'm going to bring her back to my room," Kia told the nurse.

"Are you sure, Kia? I'll be watching her and a good night's sleep is what you need."

"I only have her for a short time. I can catch up on my sleep later."

"It might be best, Kia," the nurse said softly, "if you began separating from her now. You're just going to make it harder on yourself."

"I'll take that chance," Kia said, placing Brenna in her bassinet and pushing it toward the door.

The nurse put the other baby in its bed and opened the

door for Kia. She frowned as she watched her pass through, but said, "All the best, Kia. I'll be thinking of you."

Kia turned back. "Thanks." She pushed the bassinet past the nurses' station and into her room, but she didn't climb into bed. Instead, she lifted Brenna out and then stepped back into the hallway. The coast was clear.

~

On the sixth floor, Kia padded silently down the hallway until she came to Grace's room. She peeked in, expecting to find Grace asleep, but even in the darkened room Kia could see the bed was empty. She felt a pang of alarm.

"Hi, Kia. I've been expecting you."

Kia peered into the corner. There was Grace, sitting in her wheelchair.

"Grace! What are you doing? You scared me!"

"I've been enjoying the full moon and thinking of you." Her eyes settled on the bundle in Kia's arms. "Ahh. You brought her. I was hoping you would."

Kia moved closer to the old woman. "Let me take a peek," Grace said.

Kia bent down and showed Grace the sleeping baby.

Grace smiled, and Kia was relieved to see it was the same old smile, strong and beautiful. "She's every bit as perfect as I knew she would be. Hold her closer so I can smell her."

Kia did as she was asked and Grace inhaled deeply. "There's nothing purer than that," she said. "It stirs up such beautiful memories." They gazed quietly at the sleeping baby for a few more moments. "And how are you?"

"I'm okay. But how come you're not in bed?"

"My back was sore tonight. I'd been lying flat for too many hours. I just had to get up. I'm sure someone will be here any minute to put me back in bed, but for now I'm enjoying the change of position."

Kia nodded. She sat on the edge of the bed. "We've named her Brenna Grace," she said.

Grace stared at Kia. "Really?"

Kia nodded.

Grace wiped her eyes. "I don't know what to say."

"Don't say anything, Grace."

They sat smiling at each other, their eyes filled with tears.

"I was hoping you'd come tonight," Grace said finally. "I wanted to see you with my own eyes and know that you are okay. And now I can see that you are."

"Oh, Grace. What about you? Are you okay?"

"I feel very peaceful, Kia. I really do. And look at that moon. Isn't it lovely?"

Kia nodded.

"Makes you feel like dancing, doesn't it?"

Kia could see the twinkle in Grace's eyes. As sick as she was, Grace hadn't lost her sense of humor. Kia decided to play along. "Then why don't we?" she said. Standing up, she went over and carefully propped Brenna in the old lady's lap. Then she moved around behind the wheelchair and gripped the handles. She pushed Grace and Brenna closer to the window, gently rocking the chair, like a slow dance.

"We need some music to dance to, Grace."

"Perhaps you could sing something, Kia."

"Are you kidding? Then you'd really get sick."

"Try me."

Kia looked out at the night. The soft light of the moon poured into the small room. The words to a song began to float into her head. She began to hum. Gently, she rocked the wheelchair and sang, very softly, "When universal mysteries, bring wonder in the night, creating peace and harmony, I'll hold your spirit tight." Kia cleared her throat and laughed self-consciously. "I warned you, didn't I, Grace?"

"It's a beautiful song, Kia. Don't stop."

Kia hesitated, swallowed hard, rocked the wheelchair some more and continued. "We'll seek the full moon rising, like music from above, then dance to the beat of friendship, a lullaby of love."

She had to stop again. It was a struggle to hold back the tears. She wished she'd chosen a different song.

"Keep going, Kia, please," Grace pleaded.

So Kia continued, ignoring the warble in her voice. "We'll whirl and sway together, until all dreams come true, before our souls unite in peace, my heart will dance for you."

When she was finished, Kia slowly moved around to the front of the wheelchair and picked up Brenna.

"That was beautiful." There were tears streaming down Grace's cheeks now. "That will be our song, okay, Kia? When I'm gone and you're looking out at the night sky, think of me, won't you? And sing that song."

Kia allowed her own tears to spill. She held Brenna tightly and leaned over, placing her cheek against Grace's, allowing their tears to mingle. "I will, Grace," she said. "I really will. It will always be our song. I promise."

Kia woke up the next morning to Brenna's urgent cries and was startled to see someone leaning over the bassinet, poking the tiny baby's heel with a needle.

"What are you doing to her?" she asked, alarmed. She quickly sat up, trying to clear her head.

"Just taking blood," the lab-coated woman said. "A standard procedure."

Kia lay back and watched. She couldn't believe how callous the lab technician seemed. Brenna was wailing, but the woman kept right on squeezing her heel. When she was done she bundled her back up and handed her to Kia.

"It's okay, Brenna," Kia said. "All done." The baby stared at her, eyes wide, before her bottom lip poked out into a pout and she began to cry again. Kia climbed off the bed and began to rock her. She picked up her watch that lay on the side table. It wasn't even seven o'clock, but she could hear the bustle of activity in the hall. The day had begun and she wasn't ready to face it.

Exhausted, Kia sat on the edge of her bed. Brenna continued fussing in her arms. She'd fallen asleep when she'd returned to her room last night, but Brenna woke her a short time later. She'd been hungry again, and then hadn't wanted to go back to sleep after her bottle. Each time Kia had laid her down, she began to fuss and cry. Kia had had to keep talking to her or rocking her to keep her quiet. Finally, three hours later, she'd taken another bottle and had drifted off, but had woken Kia up once more in the early hours of the morning for yet another bottle. That had only been about an hour and half ago.

Kia's breakfast tray arrived a few minutes later, so she tried placing the baby in the bassinet while she ate, but that started another round of crying and thrashing. She tried to eat while holding the baby in one arm, but after a few attempts to get her food to her mouth without spilling it on the baby she gave up. She felt too tired and nauseous to eat anyway. As she pushed the tray of food away, she saw the figure watching her from the doorway.

"Derek." Her heart banged in her chest. "What are you doing here?"

"Someone named Sadie phoned me," he said, "and told me I had to come and sign some papers." Derek was staring at the bundle in her arms. His eyes never met hers.

"Oh," she said. "I don't know anything about that."

"She said she'd meet me here."

"I haven't seen her yet today."

Derek nodded. "I might be a few minutes early."

There was a long painful moment with only Brenna's little fussing noises breaking the stillness in the room.

"So that's her?"

"Yeah. Her name's Brenna. Brenna Grace."

"She's got your hair." He stepped into the room but didn't get too close to the bed.

"Yeah, and she's got your eyes."

"Really?" He stepped a little closer.

"She doesn't bite. Come and see."

Derek hesitated. Kia could see the indecision that flickered across his face, but finally he stepped up to the bed, leaned over and peered at the little face. Kia watched as Brenna looked directly back at him. He studied her, but didn't say anything. Finally he stepped back and looked at Kia for the first time. "She's kind of cute, you know, for a newborn."

"Yeah."

"So how are you?"

Kia was startled by the question. "I'm okay, I guess. An abortion would have been way easier, but …"

He nodded.

"Her adoptive parents are really cool. You'd like them."

"That's good." He was back to studying Brenna again.

There was another long silence. Finally, Derek spoke. "I'm sorry about everything, you know?"

"Yeah. Me too." She glanced at him but quickly looked away when she saw the confusion in his eyes.

"I was really pissed off," he said. "And I've got a bad temper."

"I can be kind of pig-headed too."

"I noticed." He almost smiled. "But thanks for, you know, not saying anything. My dad never heard."

Kia nodded. Brenna was fussing again, so she put her on her shoulder and patted her back. "Do you want to hold her?"

"No!" He jerked away from the bed, crashing into Sadie as she came into the room.

"Hi," she said, stretching out her hand to shake his as he swung around. She put her other hand to her nose, which had made contact with his head. "You must be Derek. I'm Sadie."

～

When the paperwork was complete and Sadie had left,

Derek approached the bassinet where Brenna now lay sleeping peacefully.

"I have a daughter," he said, staring down at her.

Kia just nodded.

"Are you going to be okay?"

She tried to smile, but she felt her mouth tremble. "Yeah." She drew in a long breath and then let it out. "Are you?"

"Yeah." He nodded, still staring at the sleeping baby. "Why wouldn't I be?"

The room was quiet.

"Well, I guess I'll be seeing you around," he said, still not making eye contact with her.

"Yeah, I guess." Kia wished he'd hurry up and leave, it was so awkward, but he just stood there, staring at Brenna. Finally, she watched in amazement as he brought two fingers to his mouth, kissed them, then brushed the tips softly over Brenna's cheek. Then, after one more long look, he abruptly turned and left the hospital room. Kia lay back on her bed and closed her eyes. She was so tired …

❧

Justin and Kia, who was holding Brenna, stood on one side of a small table in the front of the tiny hospital chapel. Joanna and Brett stood on the other side, holding hands. Kia's parents sat in the only pew in the room, looking on.

The Reverend glanced at both couples, and when he saw they were ready, he lit a tapered candle and held it over the chalice that stood in the center of the table. "I light this candle," he said in his warm, deep voice, "to mark the arrival of the bright new spirit of Brenna and to note the love and concern shared for her well-being by all of us in this room. It is our task to make her world a better place and to do all we can to see she is raised with love and support.

"This is a day of mixed emotions," he continued, "and of confused feelings. It is a day of joy and of sadness, of dreams realized, of hard decisions made and," his voice lowered, "of grief. We must be as gentle with one another's hearts as we are with this newborn infant.

"Kia," he said, turning to face her. "You have made the hard and painful choice to give your baby into the care of others to raise as their own in your place, believing that this is the best decision for her and for you. Are you ready to do this?"

Kia looked down at the sleeping baby in her arms. The collar of the pale yellow sleeper that Joanna had brought to take her home in poked out from beneath the tightly wrapped receiving blanket. Kia had tried to comb flat the fuzzy mass of black hair, but it was already sticking out all over. She tried to blink back her tears and could feel herself shaking. She drew the baby in, squeezing her tightly, afraid of what might come out if she opened her mouth. She knew what she was supposed to say, what she had to say, but she couldn't say it. Finally, she just nodded.

She felt Justin's arm around her shoulder. She sank against him.

"Joanna and Brett," the minister continued, turning to the other couple. "You have gone through years of heartbreak and hope in trying to start your family. Until now a child has been a dream, a vision for you both. Today this dream becomes a reality with all its joys, but also with all of its awesome responsibilities. Are you ready to accept this child into your care and raise her as your own?"

This time there was no hesitation. "We are," they said with one strong voice.

"Kia." The Reverend turned back to her. "Do you have anything you wish to say to your daughter or to her new parents?"

Kia nodded. She turned slowly and handed the baby to Justin. She noticed he held her confidently, as if he'd been among babies all his life. She picked up her journal, which she'd placed beside the flickering candle, and faced the couple standing across the table from her. "For the past eight months," she told them, her soft voice trembling, "I have been keeping a journal. It describes all the feelings I've had about being pregnant and about my decision to put Brenna up for adoption." Kia paused, took a deep breath and let it out. "I didn't know that my entries had any purpose," she continued, "but the night before she was born I skimmed through it and realized it was for her. I want to give it to you now, for safekeeping, and when you think Brenna is old enough to understand, please give it to her from me. I think it will help her understand what I've been through and why I gave her to you. My final entry is a letter to her."

Kia cleared her throat, took another deep breath and read from the journal.

Tomorrow is your 'birth' day. We will finally meet face to face, even though I already feel like I know you. I have never felt a love like this before.

You will be going home with Joanna and Brett and I

believe their love for you is every bit as strong as mine. They want you as badly as I do. Their love must feel different than mine, for you are a part of me, and loving you is really like loving myself, but their love is just as real.

I know they will make excellent parents. After all, I chose them especially for you. You'll know from reading this journal that giving you away is not what I wanted to do, but what I had to do, for your sake. It is the best thing for you, even though it doesn't feel like the best thing for me right now. My hope is that you'll learn wisdom, compassion and love from Joanna and Brett, for they have so much of it to offer.

I will love you always, little daughter.
Your mom,
Kia.

Kia closed the journal, placed it on the table and looked up to see Joanna wipe a tear off her cheek. Brett nodded, his eyes shining.

"Joanna and Brett," the Reverend continued. "Do you have anything you'd like to say to Kia?"

They looked at each other and nodded. Justin was still cradling the baby, so they each reached across the table and took one of Kia's hands, forming a triangle. Brett spoke first. "We know you're taking a tremendous leap of faith by entrusting us with Brenna, Kia. In doing so, our lives become entwined in the most intimate sense and you will always be a valued and treasured part of all our lives."

Joanna continued. "Brett and I find it hard to describe to you the depth of our desire to love and raise Brenna, Kia, and how completely she will be cherished.

We thank you, deeply, for giving us this opportunity."

Kia nodded solemnly. She reached out for Brenna. Justin kissed the baby's cheek and then, reluctantly, returned her to Kia's arms. She too leaned over and kissed the tiny face.

"Kia," Reverend Petrenko said. He paused, and in that moment Kia felt a horrendous wave of sorrow wash over her. She held the baby as tightly as she safely could. "I now invite you to give Brenna to her new parents."

Although Kia was fully prepared for those words, the pain still cut right through her. She hugged the baby to her chest one last time and then, willing herself to put one foot in front of the other, she walked around the table and, very slowly, handed her to Joanna. Their eyes met and held. Then, somehow, Kia managed to get back to the other side of the table before collapsing into Justin arms. He held her close to him and she sobbed quietly into his chest.

The Reverend's voice rose above the noise of her crying. "Spirit of Life," he said. "Be with us in this time of joy and sorrow, of gladness and grief. Be with Kia as she comes to terms with the courageous choice she has made. Help her through her physical and spiritual recovery, giving her the comfort and peace of knowing she has made the best choice possible in a difficult situation. Walk with her as she returns to her life and help her realize her full potential as the fine young woman she is.

"Be with Brett and Joanna too, Spirit," he continued, "as they take on the awesome and wondrous responsibility of raising a child. Help them find strength and love in each other, reminding them to keep their marriage strong and vibrant. Be with them too as they continue to dedicate themselves to the raising of this child. May their sacrifices be born lightly in the face of their joy.

"And finally, Spirit," he said, "be with little Brenna as she learns about this vast and wonderful world. May her life be filled with laughter and love, and may her occasional tears only serve to make the joys seem all that more wonderful."

There was a long pause, during which only Kia's ragged intakes of breath could be heard in the tiny chapel.

"Kia, Justin, Brett and Joanna," the Reverend concluded, looking at each person as he said their name, "we are blessed with the presence of Brenna and her renewal of our human family. Let us carry the joy of her presence deep in our hearts to support us as we return to the world. Amen."

Kia had stopped sobbing but still had her face pressed into Justin's chest. The minister came and placed one hand on each of their shoulders. "Do you want to say goodbye, Kia?" he asked quietly.

She shook her head and held tightly onto Justin. Then she felt two hands gently touch her back before she heard footsteps leaving the tiny chapel. Brenna cried out just as the door shut behind the new family.

Kia stood with Justin for a long time, then pulled herself away and sat in the narrow space on the pew that her parents had created between them. They each put an arm around her. Eventually she sat back and wiped her eyes with the palms of both hands. Justin had come and sat beside them. He pulled off his glasses and wiped his own eyes. Her father blew his nose and her mom dabbed at her eyes with a tissue. Kia stared at the flickering candle and slowly felt her ragged breathing return to normal. She noticed that Joanna and Brett had taken the journal. They had understood.

The minister had followed the new parents out of the chapel. Kia was grateful that no one was trying to cheer her up. She didn't want to be cheered. She wanted to face the pain, to feel it deeply. Finally she stood up, went back to the table and blew out the flame. Her arms felt achingly empty and she longed to feel the movements of a baby deep inside her again. She remembered Sadie telling her that many girls who give their babies up for adoption go out and quickly become pregnant again. Kia now understood why. The sense of loss and loneliness was unbearably intense.

"Let's go," she said, starting toward the door.

They left the chapel together. Justin took her hand and they all returned to the fourth floor to collect Kia's things from her hospital room. "I want to go upstairs and see Grace," Kia said, "Just for a moment."

Her father pressed the button for the sixth floor, and when they arrived she and Justin walked down the quiet corridor to Grace's room. Kia peeked in her room and saw that the old woman was sleeping. She went back to the nurses' station, borrowed a piece of paper and pen and wrote a note.

Our dance in the moonlight was special, Grace. I will always remember it.

> *Brenna's gone to live with Joanna and Brett.*

She hesitated and then added one last thought.

I'm gonna be fine. Love you lots.
K.

Kia left the note on Grace's table. She took one last look at the old face and quietly blew her a kiss. Then she and Justin got back on the elevator with her parents.

Kia's dad pressed the button for the main floor, but the elevator stopped first at the fourth floor. Another family stepped into the car. A complete family, Kia noted. The father was carrying the new baby in a car seat while the mother stood proudly beside them. The grandparents were buried under armfuls of flowers and balloons. The four of them were positively glowing, and they barely glanced at Kia, Justin or her mom and dad, who shuffled quietly to the rear of the elevator to make room for the newcomers. Kia felt that wave of emptiness wash over her again. She clenched her teeth and fought to hold back a fresh onslaught of tears. Her dad pulled a handkerchief out of his pocket and dabbed at his red-rimmed eyes again, then her mother took the hanky out of his hand and wiped her own eyes.

It seemed like forever, but the elevator door finally opened into the lobby and the four of them stepped out.

From: Justin <justintime@yahoo.com>
To: Kia <hazelnut@hotmail.com>
Date: Aug. 21
Subject: T.O.Y.
hi kia,
all the seniors say hi and they want to know when you're coming back. i told them you'd be back when you're ready. i'm thinking of you lots.

chin up.
J

From: Justin <justintime@yahoo.com>
To: Kia <hazelnut@hotmail.com>
Date: Aug. 23
Subject: Still T.O.Y.

hi kia,
i talked to your mom last nite. i'm sure she told u. i can
understand that u don't want visitors right now. she tells me
you're all going out to the lake for a few days for a change
of scenery. call me when u get back. i hope the weather
holds 4 u.

hugs,
J.

From: Justin <justintime@yahoo.com>
To: Kia <hazelnut@hotmail.com>
Date: Aug. 28
Subject: hey you!

hi kia, are u back? did u catch any fish?
the seniors' are going 2 hijack a bus and come over and
storm your house if u don't come by for a visit soon.
ps. is the nausea gone?

J

From: Justin <justintime@yahoo.com>
To: Kia <hazelnut@hotmail.com>
Date: Aug. 30
Subject: bbq

hi ki, the youth group is having an end-of-summer barbecue
at my house at 4:00 on sept. 6th, rain or shine. it's going 2
be fun, but it won't be the same without u, so please,
please come. i can't predict what might happen if you don't

show. the group just might land on your doorstop, barbecue and all, so u might as well come.

J

ps. have u heard from joanna and brett? how is she doing?

From: Kia <hazelnut@hotmail.com>
To: Justin <justintime@yahoo.com>
Date: Aug. 30
Subject: Re: bbq

justin, they've been calling constantly. she's fine. i told them
to stop calling for awhile. it hurts too much.

k

From: Justin <justintime@yahoo.com>
To: Kia <hazelnut@hotmail.com>
Date: Aug. 30
Subject: hallelujah!!!!!!!!!!!!!!

o kia. it was such a relief 2 hear from u. please write some
more. it will help to talk about it.

J

From: Kia <hazelnut@hotmail.com>
To: Justin <justintime@yahoo.com>
Date: Sept. 2
Subject: sorry

it's just too much effort. everything is. i'll write when i can.

k

week 40/40

Aug. 27
It's been two weeks, two weeks of pain. All I want to do
is sleep and forget, but when I sleep I feel like I'm
falling,
falling,
falling
and I wake up with a jolt.
Will it ever end?

Kia smiled shyly at her friends from Youth Group when she arrived late for the end-of-summer barbecue at Justin's house. They looked amazed to see her.

"My God, Kia, look at you," Meagan said. "You're, like, *so* skinny!"

"Getting there," she answered, looking down at her loose sundress.

"I'm glad you came," Justin said. Kia could see the sincerity of those words in the way he was looking at her. The rush of feelings she still had for him almost overwhelmed her.

"I wasn't going to."

"What made you change your mind?"

"I've got to face school in two days," she said, looking away. "I figured coming here might be the best way to break into real life again."

"Good plan."

She shrugged and then sat beside Justin in the circle they had formed on the grass. A chalice with a flickering candle stood in the center.

"So, we've each had a turn describing what we did this summer, Kia," he said, "and then we shared what we learned about ourselves from those experiences."

"And it's your turn, Justin," Meagan reminded him.

"I was hoping you'd forget," he said, looking around the group. Everyone's eyes were on him. He took a deep breath, and let it out slowly. "Okay," he said. "I've had the most ... the most amazing summer of my life." He stretched out his legs, making himself more comfortable. "First of all, I witnessed birth, the birth of Kia's baby. It was incredible." He looked down at her, but she wouldn't make eye contact with him. "I can only describe it as ... powerful. Totally. I think it's changed the way I look at life, and it's definitely confirmed my belief in some kind of higher power, or force, call it whatever you want. There's no way that perfect new baby could be just a fluke of nature."

Justin looked around the group, expecting a reaction, but they all regarded him solemnly.

"What else happened, Justin? You said 'first of all.' What is second of all?" Meagan asked.

"Second of all ..." Justin swallowed and pulled his legs up so that he was sitting cross-legged. He looked down at his hands, folded in his lap. "Well, second of all,

I've decided to come out, publicly." He looked up. "And proudly."

"Come out?" Chris asked.

"That's right," Justin said, looking up and meeting Chris's eyes. "I'm gay."

There was a moment of complete silence, and then Meagan asked, "What made you decide to come out now?"

Justin looked down at Kia, and then put his arm around her shoulder. "Kia did."

She looked up, startled. "I did?"

"Yeah," he said.

"No, I didn't."

"You didn't have to say anything," he said. "But I watched and admired how you handled being pregnant. You were so brave."

Brave, Kia thought. The same word Grace had used to describe her.

"And I thought if you could be so brave, why couldn't I?"

"How long have you known you were gay?" Laurel asked.

"Quite a long time. And my parents know, and so does the Rev and a few other people, but I just haven't been able to talk about it openly before." He looked around at the serious faces.

The teens looked at each other and then back at Justin. "So?" Laurel asked. "What's the big deal?"

There were nods and shrugs around the circle.

Justin smiled. "I knew you guys would be cool, but it feels like such a relief to say it out loud anyway."

"Group hug!" declared Meagan, and they all got to their feet, pushed Justin into the center of the circle and hugged him together. Then, laughing, they returned to the circle on the grass.

Justin studied Kia's face as the group grew serious again. "So, Kia," he said, "that leaves you. Are you ready to tell us about your summer?"

"Yeah, I guess," she said in a voice not much louder than a whisper. "Though everyone already knows what I did." She patted her almost flat stomach.

"Tell us anyway," he said softly, "in your own words."

Kia sat quietly, collecting her thoughts, and then she turned and gave Justin a small, teasing smile. There was a flicker of mischief in her eyes. She started to speak, as if from rote, "What I did on my summer vacation. On my summer vacation I had a baby."

"That's it?" he asked, a matching flicker in his own eyes. "Nothing interesting?"

"Nope, that's about it. Oh, yeah," she said, perking up. "I volunteered at the seniors' home too. And I made a new friend." Her shoulders sagged suddenly and she dropped her head. Her long hair hung around her face and she added quietly, "But she's sick."

"So," Justin said, gently placing a hand on her shoulder. He tilted his head and tried to look into her face, but it was hidden behind her hair. "What have you learned about yourself from all this?"

Kia sat very still. It was a long time before she spoke, and when she did, the others had to strain to hear the words. "I learned to dance naked," she whispered, looking up into the surprised faces of her friends. "And so did you, Justin," she said, turning just in time to see his look of astonishment. She continued, speaking a little louder. "And I learned that I'm not as selfish as I thought I was. A selfish person might have kept Brenna. I let her go because it was the best thing for her."

"What was it like … giving her away?" Laurel asked softly.

Kia swallowed hard. "It was hell. It's still hell. I can't see a baby on the street or on TV without bawling my eyes out. I cry myself to sleep almost every night." She blinked hard. "I even cry when I see dog food," she said with a small laugh, but then grew serious again. "I feel so empty. For nine months I had a baby growing inside me. Now there's nothing." She paused, and then continued. "I don't know if I'll ever get over it. I love her to death. If I had to give up my life for her, I'd do it in a heartbeat."

Everyone sat very still. There was a clap of thunder in the distance.

"If you had to do it all again," Chris asked, "would you choose abortion next time?"

Kia thought about that. "It's weird to think that if I'd gone through with it, with the abortion," she said, "there'd be no Brenna. I'm sure an abortion would've been way, way easier, but I think what I did was the right thing for me. Actually, I know it was. I'm glad I was able to give Joanna and Brett a child and it was awesome to find out what my body could do—grow a baby and all that. But I'll never be the same." She sighed, then looked up at the gathering storm clouds. "I feel like I've aged about twenty years. I've lost my … my youth, I guess. Just being a teenager. I really regret that. No," she said, shaking her head, "if I had to do it all over again I'd just make sure I didn't get pregnant in the first place."

"Is there anything else you've learned?" Justin asked.

"Yeah," she said, looking around at the group. "I've learned who my friends are."

"And who are they?" he asked.

"The people who stick with you no matter what. Like you guys."

Justin nodded.

There was a flash of lightning in the far distance, followed by another rumble of thunder, but no one moved.

"Who is your friend that is sick?" Mike asked, ignoring the large drops of rain that were beginning to fall on them.

"An old woman from the seniors' home," she answered. "Grace, or Graceful, as we all call her. I haven't known her long, but she's really special. She's the one who told me about dancing naked."

"Did she really mean you should do that?" Chris asked, puzzled.

Kia thought about it. "Yes and no." She strained to remember the conversation she'd had with Grace not so many weeks ago. "I think she felt we should try to get our minds and bodies to work, or dance, more in unison." She shook her head and added quietly, "If my head and body had been working as a team, I wouldn't have become pregnant in the first place."

There were a few nods.

"And she says that when we make tough decisions, and go with them, it's like dancing naked. You expose yourself to others—just like Justin did tonight."

He picked up her hand.

"And really," Kia smiled, "don't you think dancing naked would make you feel like ... really alive? I think that was her point too."

"Yeah," Chris laughed. "Especially if it was cold outside."

Justin grinned down at her. "Maybe there'll be a full moon tonight," he said, "after the storm passes, and...."

"Hey, I'm outta here if that's the plan," Mike said.

Justin nodded. "Okay, then it can be Kia's solo."

"Forget it, I've got stretch marks." Kia laughed and realized, with shock, that she hadn't really laughed in weeks. It felt good.

"Whatever," Chris said. "It's about to pour. Let's move."

"Yeah," Mike agreed, looking up. "And let's eat. I'm starved."

Kia realized she was hungry too, but it actually felt good to feel something other than pain again.

Justin joined hands with Kia and Mike, and everyone else followed suit, holding hands with their immediate neighbors, until the circle was completely linked. Leaning forward, Justin blew out the candle. "The flame will be gone but the memories linger," he recited.

"We carry the light," the group chanted in return. "We carry the warmth."

"So be it," Justin said.

With a final squeeze of hands, the circle was broken and the group moved to the sheltered space under the second-floor sundeck. Justin lit the barbecue and they watched as the storm moved in.

Later, Kia sat off to one side of the group, alone but

content. The storm had passed and kindling was being arranged in a firepit.

"Kia," Justin said, joining her. "Look!" He pointed at something over her shoulder.

She turned to see what it was. A perfect rainbow arched across the eastern sky.

"The universal sign of hope," she said quietly, remembering the half-rainbow they'd seen together last winter.

Justin just nodded, and they watched, in awe, as the individual colors shimmered in the unusual light.

"I've never seen anything quite like it," Kia said finally. "It's perfect."

Justin nodded, and rested his hand on her shoulder. "And I'd say that if you believe in signs, or messages from the universe, this would be one."

She looked at him thoughtfully, then turned back to the rainbow. A sign of hope. She'd hang on to that thought.

~

Kia pulled on the jeans she hadn't worn in eight months. She sucked in her stomach and then tugged at the zipper. It pulled straight up. She grinned, admiring herself in the mirror. Downstairs, she grabbed her book bag and headed out the door. Shawna was waiting at the corner.

"This is the first day of our last year of high school," Shawna commented as they walked toward the old school building. "Party time!"

Kia nodded, but didn't answer.

Shawna glanced at her. "Why don't we have a make-over party on Friday night? For old times' sake."

Kia smiled. "Sounds great, Shawn, but Friday night

and Saturday I'm volunteering at the seniors' home."

"Really?" Shawna asked, astonished. "Don't you already have, like, way too many community service points?"

"I do," Kia nodded.

Shawna shook her head, but her smile was warm. "It's great to have you back, Kia. I've missed you."

"I've missed you too, Shawn," Kia said, knowing exactly what Shawna meant. It had been a long and sometimes lonely detour, but Justin was right. With her eyes wide open, it had been an amazing journey.

epilogue

The light from the full moon illuminates the trees standing strong and dignified at the edge of the forest. She is one with them, exposed to the elements without fear, without shame. The music of the universe drums inside her head, inside her heart. She lifts her outstretched arms to the night sky, feeling her spirit surge through her entire being, reborn, alive. It rushes down her arms to her fingertips, down her legs to her toes. With complete abandon she twirls around and around, the cool night air licking at her bare skin, the spongy, damp grass the perfect dance floor.

As she dances she peels off the remaining garb of her past, the attire that is no longer her. She is still a daughter, still a mother, but now she will wear the strong fabric of self-knowledge, fashioning a new identity, one that is both innocent and wise, sensitive and resilient.

She dances, and as she dances, the spirit of Grace joins her. They dance together, wild and free.